TREASURE OF
THE GENERAL GRANT

BRIAN WILSON

DEDICATION

I would like to dedicate this book to a good friend, Keith Shand, who passed away in January 2019. I have missed the monthly chats over coffee in which we attempted to resolve the world's problems. As a friend, I dearly valued his integrity, honesty and loyalty. Keith wrote the biography in my last book, *The First Trumpet*. As a writer, it was a bonus to have a friend like him who I could count on to offer an honest opinion on my book drafts.

Other books by Brian Wilson

SHORT STORIES

Moments in Time

A collection of short stories, 2012

Bumpy Roads

A collection of short stories, 2013

Here Comes the Sun-Perhaps?

A collection of short stories, 2015

So that's Life?

A collection of short stories, 2016

NOVELS

Operation Iran, 2016

The First Trumpet, 2017

ACKNOWLEDGEMENTS

In writing this novel I have been encouraged by the ongoing support and feedback from family, friends and other readers.

I would also like to thank those readers who have taken time to write honest reviews of my book on the Internet. For a writer, such reviews are important and provide the necessary feedback and incentive to keep on writing.

My Facebook page is https://www.facebook.com/brianwilsonauthor

My Website: https://www.brian-d-wilson.com/

Prologue

"What the heck?

Out of the haze land suddenly appeared like a cloud over their heads, but it was too late for the 179-foot clipper and the 83 onboard. The General Grant now trapped in the choppy swell was being drawn in on a kamikaze course towards the rugged cliffs. It was futile; nothing could be done in these light winds to steer the ship away from the jagged rocks. The crew and passengers could just hopelessly watch on and contemplate their fate as the ship drifted nearer and nearer to the largest of these desolate wind-torn islands which had, over the years, claimed many lives and accounted for many wreckages.

The night had been cloudy, very dark and wet; too dark to see in time the outline of the largest of the Auckland Islands looming up in the near distance. It was totally unexpected, given the gentle passage and good progress the General Grant had made since leaving Melbourne on the 4th of May 1866. Now to see their dreams of reaching London shattered and to be left to dwell on the prospect of, at best, being stranded in this cold sub-Antarctic area, seemed incomprehensible. For the crew and passengers this inconceivable irony (a tragedy occurring in calm conditions, in an area otherwise known for its gales and violent seas) made very little sense.

Boom!

Finally, in the early hours of the 14th of May 1866, the 1005 ton, American built clipper slammed headfirst into the cliffs losing her fore-boom-staysail. She then bounced astern and drifted for half a mile scraping along the cliff face, losing her rudder in the process, before being swallowed up into a large cave of two hundred and fifty yards in length. This deep dark tomb was to be her resting place, and grave for some of those on board.

Snap!

The mizzen-mast broke as it smashed against the roof of the cave and fell headlong onto the boat. But this was only the start as the tide had not yet finished with the General Grant. Overnight it continued to rise and smash the clipper against the jagged rocks, eventually wedging the main mast under the roof of the cave. As the tide rose the mast was forced downwards like a spear, finally penetrating the hull and inviting the sea in to claim its prize. The crew and passengers now had no choice but to take to the lifeboats as the ship weighed heavily in the now turbulent waters. First, the two-quarter boats left the sinking ship with nine crew and six passengers safely reached land. The remaining crew and passengers in the much larger lifeboat were not so lucky, their boat swamped with water shortly after leaving the General Grant. Unfortunately, most of these people drowned."

"And the captain?"

"No, he went down with the ship, Robbie."

"Eventually, the ship sunk with its cargo of wool and skins, 2,576 ounces of gold, and nine tons of zinc spelter, a generous bounty for any treasure hunter brave or fool-hardy enough to venture into such dangerous and inhospitable waters."

Uncle rose from the edge of my bed.

"Time to go to sleep Robbie, you have school tomorrow."

"But what happened to the treasure, Uncle Henry?" I asked.

"Never you mind about that treasure my lad. Go to sleep Robbie, it's past your bedtime," my uncle replied with a glint in his eyes.

Chapter 1

"For where your treasure is, there your heart will be also."

Luke 12:34

The deathly silence and empty corridors were unnerving; it was as though I was entering a haunted house, but here I might finally receive a long-awaited answer to my question concerning the General Grant. Maybe this was just a rest home but for me, it was one of the dullest and morbid of places. There was not a single person in sight, just silence and emptiness, as I made my way down a long empty corridor where every step echoed, reminding me that I was nearing 50, and one day this might also be my home. Perhaps the Grim Reaper had visited already and cleared out the place of spent lives in preparation for the next generation of nervous and unwitting arrivals. Wasn't this after-all, a station where people waited to depart to some unknown destination?

I was eventually reassured that there was in fact life in this morbid place as I passed the TV room, the aired programme a loud welcome to this deathly silence. It was a room buzzing with activity with even a tropical fish tank bubbling away in one corner; the normally placid Angelfish in a feeding frenzy as a guppy was giving birth. The noise in the room challenged every negative preconception I had believed of this place. These residents, far from morose and incapacitated, were heartily engaged passing away their remaining days or hours watching TV, reading books and newspapers or knitting. These weren't people waiting to die but rather people intent on savouring every remaining precious minute. They had come to appreciate the finitude of life; time in the past so thoughtlessly wasted. To think that within this one room there was a library of knowledge with memories dating back decades and secrets and truths about the past that might be lost forever, buried in the sands of time. This was my greatest concern as I wondered about the General Grant and proceeded down the corridor to my uncle's room.

My Uncle Henry was one of those people who guarded many secrets and answers to mysteries. It was most likely that these might all be taken to his grave, as he was very tight-lipped when treasure was involved. Mention the General Grant and he would immediately change the subject and retell one of his adventures, though not giving away too many details. At one time a colourful character: explorer, treasure-hunter, adventure seeker and archaeologist of sorts, he now looked grey and at death's door as he sat slumped and motionless in a sturdy wooden chair that would hardly have contributed anything to his comfort. Saliva dripped from each corner of his mouth as he stared blankly at the bare wall in front. I entered his bedroom, which was somewhat clinical in appearance and devoid of pictures or favourite possessions. This was how my uncle wanted it as he saw his stay here as unwanted and temporary. He remained unfazed, seemingly in a catatonic state without even a twitch of an eyelid.

"Uncle Henry?" My uncle didn't budge, nor did he acknowledge my presence. He remained still as if rigor mortis had already set in.

"Uncle?"

"Get me out of here," he pleaded, without turning or lifting his head. "How dare they treat me like a caged animal?"

"But Uncle, you're 85 and you keep having blackouts. You're here for your own good and need to have nurses around to keep an eye on you at all times," I replied.

My uncle reluctantly nodded. "Still I'd rather be dead than sit here like a stuffed dummy counting my remaining hours. This is torture. There's nothing left in life for me now except death. Sadly, my adventures have come to a cruel end but to die here in these dreary surroundings is most undignified. If I am to die I'd rather do so falling off a mountain, or into a crevasse, or at the hands of some undiscovered tribesmen in the deep Amazon jungle, but certainly not this way."

"Or diving for treasure, maybe the General Grant's," I added.

"Treasure's nothing but trouble, Robbie. If you find it, then believe me, it is best to say nothing," said Uncle. "Tell no one. All it brings is trouble."

"So it's true then that you found the General Grant's treasure?"

"Did I say that, Robbie?" He slowly lifted and turned his head and glared at me with his bloodshot blue eyes underlined by deep dark bags. "Four days I've been here and not one person has come. Not one person. Even the animals in the zoo get more visitors and probably better food."

"I'm sorry," I replied. "I caught a nasty bug and the last thing I wanted was to pass it on to you and give you pneumonia. Besides, Invercargill is a long way to travel to at the drop of a hat. It's not easy getting away from the farm."

"You and your damned sheep. Wasting your time on dumb animals when the world's waiting to be explored. I wish you had come and brought your bugs so I was put out of my misery." My uncle slowly brought a handkerchief to his face and on the third swipe managed to wipe away the saliva. The handkerchief slipped from his weak grip and fell onto his knees. "Damn!" he exclaimed in frustration as his shaky hand fumbled to retrieve the handkerchief. "I'm falling apart. And your wife and two sons?"

"They too were affected and are still battling it," I replied. "Unfortunately the change of season is always a bad time for cold bugs. You're lucky that this is a nice warm place."

"Take me for a drive, Robbie. I want to see the sea or the mountains," he demanded. "Anything! Just get me out of here before I go totally mad."

"I really wish I could but they said you were most unwell and needed twenty-four hours monitoring. They just won't let me. I have already asked," I lied.

"What's the point?" grumbled my uncle. "I'm dying regardless and there's no quality of life in just sitting counting the hours. You could smuggle me out. Come on, for once in your life take a risk; it's in our genes, Robbie. Surely you can give your uncle just one last adventure?"

"I would love to, Uncle, but if you were to cark it in the process it really wouldn't be a good look; I would probably be in big trouble. Besides the cold southerly outside is not the weather for a Sunday drive."

"At least one of your sons is an adventurer, a man after my own heart and he wouldn't have turned me down." Uncle paused and wiped the saliva again from the corner of his mouth. He picked up a glass of water and with a shaky hand finally found his lips, but in the process, some escaped and ran down his chin then dripped onto an already food-stained shirt. He returned the glass with a thud, misjudging the height of the table.

"Damn! Old age is no fun," he murmured. "Everything goes: your hearing, sight, coordination, knees, everything." Uncle coughed, producing a rattle in his chest.

"You know, being the oldest I could have had that farm, but that boring life was never for me, not when there's a whole world out there to explore."

"I know, Uncle, you've reminded us many times, and my dad and I are grateful. He loved the farm and the farming lifestyle."

"Strange he loved it," continued my uncle, "and I don't regret any minute of my life even if I did have many close brushes with death. I've had a great life and wouldn't change a thing, not one thing." For one moment the corner of his lips curled and a smile looked like it might surface as my uncle was obviously recalling the good old times.

"It was the excitement, Uncle, you liked the adrenalin rush and change of scenery."

"Oh yes, I believe I must have. Your father and I were chalk and cheese: he was content with just pottering on the farm whereas I needed to stretch my legs and explore the world. I've always been a restless spirit." My uncle paused and the room again became deathly silent for a few minutes.

"Didn't do your dad much good though, the farm life, considering I've outlived him by twenty years or so. All those chemicals he used on the farm wouldn't have helped. Surely you must get itchy feet now and again, and have a desire for exploration and adventure, Robbie? It's in our Scottish blood you know."

"Maybe sometimes, perhaps," I lied, "but there's plenty to keep me busy on the farm and I too love the laidback farming lifestyle. One can't just walk away and leave the animals unattended and I have a wife and two lads to support."

"Stuff those dumb smelly sheep, though I guess it's your livelihood. You've always got the lake if you run into hard times," reminded my uncle, slightly raising his head and making eye contact.

"Droughts? Nothing that bad to date but yes, that water hole could keep us going over a couple of dry years. They say that the world climate is getting warmer and drier but this is in a sense wasted land that could be put out to pasture. I had planned at some stage to drain it and do exactly that."

"Good." Uncle managed to produce almost a smile of sorts on an otherwise stolid face and for a few seconds, a little colour returned to his death-grey complexion. "Something your father talked about when he first took over the farm but sadly never got around to doing. It was your granddad's idea to flood the land and he's never needed it either."

"And at least one of my sons is keen to continue with the farm when it becomes too much for me," I continued. "But these days it's becoming harder to make a living as wool and lamb prices drop."

"Yes, you must keep the farm in the family." My uncle looked tired and had now closed his eyes. "Keeping it in the family is a good ..."

"Well, I best be going," I said, but Uncle had already drifted into sleep. He now sat there with his head cocked to one side. His breathing sounded shallow, suggesting that it wouldn't be long before he met his maker. Time was not on my side if I was to solve the mystery of the General Grant.

Mostly though, I would miss a once cheerful uncle, a great storyteller sharing his adventures. How much was true, I didn't know, as he was silent on anything that really mattered.

Chapter 2

"To the well-organized mind, death is but the next great adventure."
J.K. Rowling, Harry Potter and the Sorcerer's Stone

Shortly after my visit, Uncle died. He died in his sleep, probably while dreaming of one of his many wild adventures. Perhaps, in the end, he died as he wished, falling off a mountain, or into a crevasse, or at the hands of some tribesman's poisoned dart somewhere in the depths of the Amazon jungle.

Being his closest surviving relative it was reluctantly left for me to organise his funeral, not the most envious of tasks. I hated funerals and made every effort in the past, to the disapproval of my wife Mary, to avoid them. On the day of the funeral in Invercargill, I was greeted at death's door by the funeral director, a person not unlike Count Dracula's butler in appearance who held a similar demeanour of melancholy. Of pale complexion and dressed exquisitely in a tight-fitting black suit he extended his winter-chilled hand and dutifully offered his commiserations. The venue was my uncle's choice and not at all to my liking. I would have preferred the warmth of a spirit-filled church and the comfort of knowing that my uncle was now on a new adventure in higher places, but he had remained stubbornly agnostic and wouldn't be seen near a church.

As guests started to file in, Mary pushed me towards the door to greet each new-comer.

"It's your uncle and your job," she reminded me. "You must make people welcome."

Reluctantly I obeyed, even though shaking hands, mingling with people and making small-talk was not for me.

I didn't expect many of his friends to be turning up to an 85 year-olds funeral. Most of his generation would have long since passed away or would now be incapacitated or too frail to brave the winter southerly blast that had been sweeping up from the south off Antarctica. I predicted a light turnout of mostly our friends and neighbours.

"Sorry about your uncle," said a short plump baldish gentleman dressed smartly in a blue suit and matching tie as he extended his cold hand.

"Guess, it was his time to go as there was nothing left in this world for the old feller. Poor old Henry."

"Yes," I replied, "and you are?"

"I'm his solicitor, Tom Scott. You'll be hearing a lot from me shortly once I get his will sorted. Ah, shouldn't be too onerous a task given that you're the only beneficiary," he laughed nervously. "Just, really I don't want to go there, but ah, the tax department has been asking a lot of questions recently, which is never a good sign. Unprecedented, really, not good at all."

"Oh!" I looked shocked at the thought that my uncle may have upset the tax department.

"Never mind, we can talk later," he added, patting me on the back before walking away to give me the space to greet other guests.

While he had been talking I had noticed an older woman in her sixties, accompanied by a younger woman in her forties slip past; the older woman sneaking a cursory glance at me in the process. It soon became increasingly apparent that they were not the only ones trying to avoid eye contact and to slip past unannounced. I had anticipated, given my uncle's reputation as a treasure hunter, that maybe the odd opportunist, hoping secrets were revealed, might turn up at the funeral. These types of occasions did tend to lend themselves to good yarns and family secrets being revealed. I was also hoping to hear some myself and learn more about my uncle and who he really was.

A large hand touched my shoulder and I turned to face a tall grey-headed man in his sixties.

"Andrew Parker," said the man as he passed me a business card. "I was a diver who worked for your uncle. I live in Auckland and I know that now obviously isn't a good time, but I'd like to catch up with you sometime to discuss the General Grant."

"General Grant! Did you say the General Grant?"

"Yes, the General Grant."

"Oh most definitely," was my reply. Finally, I might now have answers on a subject which I had heard so many rumours and a topic my uncle had avoided like the plague. Perhaps these stories were true and my uncle had found the treasure, a treasure that had eluded many a salvage operation. But what a burden for me as my uncle's sole beneficiary and was this why the tax office was involved? Often my wife would call me Mr Anxiety and she had frequently chastised me over my propensity to worry. "If you continue to worry you'll die of a stomach ulcer", she had warned. As a result, I would often take a glass of antacid before going to bed as a precaution.

I continued to shake hands as a number of other people approached me, each expressing their sympathy but now my mind was elsewhere. Anxiety had taken centre stage and I pondered whether I may be inheriting a national treasure. I was now just going through the motions—auto-pilot—as I shook each hand in turn and pretended to listen and respond with a thank you. It became increasingly of concern that the onus might fall on me to correct the history books otherwise adventure seekers might continue to risk their lives and savings in search of a treasure that no longer existed. But in going public what sort of a hornet's nest might be stirred up? For instance, charities might target our phone line and mailbox once they discovered our good fortune. Another hand, this time quite warm, rested heavily on my shoulder. I turned to meet the warm, brown eyes of a strongly built elderly gentleman in his seventies.

"Gregory Brown," announced the tall man. "I was your uncle's business partner for thirty years."

"Another treasure hunter," I replied excitedly. "I look forward to catching up with you later on to hear all the war stories. There's so much I want to hear about my uncle and his adventures. I want to know more about who my uncle really was."

"Sometimes, Robbie, some things are better not spoken about, but yes, I will most definitely catch up with you later. We have a lot to talk about." Gregory Brown surreptitiously disappeared into the funeral venue which was unexpectedly quite packed.

Suffice to say during the service there were many war stories but, to the disappointment of many an opportunists, these were deliberately short on details as tight-lipped treasure-hunters recalled their conveniently vague memories of an uncle who was high spirited and flamboyant and added to the excitement of each expedition. The General Grant was unfortunately not on the conversation menu.

My uncle hadn't specified who he wanted to conduct the ceremony, so I cheekily took the liberty of inviting my local pastor from my home-town, Gore, despite my uncle's views on religion. I thought that if anything the old fellow might benefit from, it would be a prayer or two to help him on his next adventure. I thought that the pastor, quite a charismatic character, might brighten up a somewhat sad occasion.

Immediately following the service I was swamped with friends and neighbours offering their condolences, so much so that my good wife ended up having to bring me a cup of tea and a savoury. Eventually, after I was given some reprieve, I was able to go in search of food but found that the vultures had already beaten me to the tastiest items. Once again the same warm hand pressed upon my shoulder and I turned around.

"You didn't think I was going to let you get away," laughed Gregory Brown, patting me on the back, "especially when your uncle made me promise that I would keep an eye on you. He was very fond of you, you know. Not sure though that he would have approved of a pastor taking the service. Quite a character that pastor and not at all what I expected."

"Neither do I," I laughed, "but my uncle's not here to disapprove. So you're here to keep an eye on me I gather?"

"Yes, treasure-hunting is a dangerous occupation even after you've found the treasure. There's always some who think they're entitled to a portion; you know; a distant relative, government or even the tax department and of course the criminals who'd try to steal your treasure. They realise that treasure, especially ancient relics, are not easy to sell and must be hidden somewhere. Then there's your uncle's accountant and solicitor, neither of whom I would trust but your uncle couldn't be told as he was very stubborn and strong-willed. Somebody's got to look out for you to see you receive what your uncle had intended. The accountant in particu…..My God, is that Martha?"

"Sorry, Gregory?"

"Martha, your uncle's ex-girlfriend," Gregory said, pointing towards the oldest of two women sneaking out the door.

"Really! And I thought my uncle had always been celibate," I replied. "Guess she must be quite upset that he has died."

"To the contrary," laughed Gregory, "she was probably making sure that he was finally dead after he abandoned her and excluded her from a lucrative treasure hunt. My, hasn't she aged? Not the pretty little thing I once knew. I guess we're all getting older and uglier."

"So which treasure was that?" I enquired.

"You don't need to know," Gregory sharply replied. "In the treasure-hunting game the less said the safer for everyone. Anyhow, you were telling me about your family farm. Now let's see, was it a dairy farm…?"

"No, in Gore we're famous for our Romney sheep, but there are now some dairy farms in the area, Gregory. The move to dairying seems to have swept the country. We won't be going there though as it costs millions to convert to dairying. Anyhow as more farmers go to dairying, fewer sheep are farmed and lamb and mutton income goes up."

"Ah, a man with an eye to making money, my sort of man," Gregory laughed. "Well, I'm sure at some stage you'll be able to fill me in all about farming. Perhaps I can come and visit you sometime in the near future."

"You're very welcome, Gregory."

Chapter 3

"Anxiety does not empty tomorrow of its sorrows, but only empties today of its strength."
Charles Spurgeon

Over the next two weeks anxiety took centre stage and I had many sleepless nights. Mary frequently complained about my tossing and turning, as well as voicing the usual protests about my untamed talons shredding the bed-sheets and losing the blankets to me on a cold winter's night. During this unsettled period I felt lucky to not be relegated to the dining room couch; a resting place I had graced at times over the years. It was hard enough for me having lost my only uncle without now having the additional worry of problems transpiring once I received my inheritance. What was this inheritance and was it all legal?

My uncle had lived out of a suitcase and had very few personal effects that might provide answers and relieve my anxiety. An old ripped beer carton held all his important papers. Mary and I set aside one night to sift through this carton. It was an unenvious task, given the dust, cobwebs, dead flies and moths covering what my uncle had deemed important. He clearly had no interest at all in methodically filing records and instead favoured the chronological approach of just stuffing papers, receipts and forms, as they were received, into the carton. I sighed in despair as we worked our way through the box.

Mary tried to calm my nerves by reassuring me that I should feel very grateful and blessed that I was undisputedly the sole beneficiary. It hadn't been the same for Mary after her parents had died several years ago, leaving everything to her youngest brother. It had not been plain sailing as her family became bitter and divided, embroiled in an ugly dispute involving lawyers. In hindsight, it seemed absurd that money matters should divide families as they often do when the distribution of an estate is at stake. The world has never been a fair playing field and in New Zealand, like most other countries, who inherits what is always going to raise its ugly head.

In my case, I was an only child and inherited the 200-hectare farm from my father. He had thirty years earlier inherited half from his parents and purchased the other half from my uncle. This left my father with a hefty mortgage and for many years our family struggled just keeping our heads above water and the bank from the door. That was until one day when we received an unexpected surprise; a sizeable legacy from a Great Aunt Betty in England who, apart from my uncle, we never knew existed. This injection of finance came at a good time and it placed my father in such a strong financial position that he was able to not only pay off the mortgage but also purchase a third of a neighbour's farm. It was this ex-neighbours son, Colin, who I had decided to talk to in an attempt to calm my anxiety.

Colin was a police constable, somebody I thought I could confide in, who was bound to have some idea about the legality and illegality of treasure. He had recently transferred back from Auckland to his home town of Gore. When he was twelve his parents were forced to sell up and leave Gore as his father, in separating from his wife, could no longer afford to keep the farm. He avoided a mortgagee sale when my father and another neighbour chipped in to purchase their farm. I had lost track of this family and wouldn't have recognised Colin had he not introduced himself at the funeral. Now in his early forties, he was quite stocky and his black hair revealed a few grey streaks. I had arranged to meet with him at one of the few local watering holes, Traffer's pub. When I say few, Gore having a residential population of just 12,000 has few of most things even though it is the second-largest town in the province of Southland. This meeting came at a price though, a jug of beer, which I was most happy to provide and Colin more than happy to empty. I was hoping that this meeting might calm my anxiety.

"Long time no see," I said shaking his hand as he rose from the pub table. "Thank you for coming to my uncle's funeral."

"The least I could do," replied Colin. "I'm glad to be back in Gore."

"It's really great to see you after all these years, Colin. Gosh, you look just like your father. I often wondered about you and where you had gone to live. It all happened so suddenly with you and your family leaving. You've done very well for yourself getting into the police force. I've heard of so many who've been turned down and others who have had to wait for years before being accepted." I sat down at the table and started pouring a glass of beer.

"Na, nothing at all to do with merit, Robbie. When you work in a big city you realise that's not the way this world works, mate." Colin shook his head. "Got in simply because I was a Maori boy and the bosses were able to tick the boxes for equal employment. You know they must meet their quota for Maori, Pacific Islanders and so forth. Damn-right insulting and racist to be just a statistic."

"I'm sure you would have been selected on your merits, a good strongly built rural lad such as yourself."

"Sure, then why did they give me all the dirty jobs and station me in South Auckland on the beat dealing with drunks, idle thugs, and unruly Maori and Pacific Islanders? Those racist pricks never intended me to patrol the more compliant suburbs. I have to say it's been nice moving away from all that nonsense in the big smoke. At times the job felt more like being a social worker filling in for absentee and irresponsible parents. I feel quite at home now being back in Gore, even if my job does include traffic duties."

"Oh yes, I remember when the government combined the police and traffic officers allowing for more resources; well that's what they argued at the time. The police were not at all happy with the thought of traffic duties and the traffic officers were rubbing their hands with glee at the thought of higher pay."

"Agreed. Handing out speeding tickets is not my cup of tea, but in a small place like Gore, we have to be multi-skilled and do these menial tasks as well, even when you're put in the position of having to give somebody local a ticket. It doesn't do too much for your social life or standing in the community. Overall, it's much better being away from the big smoke, though it would've been nice to return to the family farm."

"I'm really glad you've returned, Colin." I gulped a mouthful of beer. "It brings back happy memories of our childhood. Shame your father had to sell up and you all moved away when we had so much fun together but the cold facts are that so many marriages these days pack up."

"Now don't get me started, Robbie. After all these years I'm still bitter about that; Mum and Dad splitting up and your parents and other neighbours exploiting the situation and snatching our farm for a song," Colin replied. "That's neighbours for you. You can't trust anyone."

"Colin, as I recall we weren't that flush ourselves at the time and it was the best my parents could offer. As I remember, my parents said that the deal was still a lot better for your dad than a mortgagee sale and being ripped off big time by the greedy banks. So you moved to Auckland then?"

"What, Auckland, on the measly farm proceeds? You've got to be joking, Robbie. A two-bedroom house in Whangarei was the best we could afford at the time," said Colin. "With the bank holding out its hand for repayment and the farm selling for a song, and a matrimonial distribution on top, my father didn't have a bean to play with."

"Well, it's good to have you back," I said. "I remember those good old days we used to play in the barn and sometimes go down to the Mataura River to fish and more."

"Yes, we did get into a lot of trouble and it was worth it," laughed Colin. "They were great days and our parents would have had a fit if they saw what we had got up to. We could easily have drowned in the river. Then there was the time we got chased by a bull."

"Yes, that was rather scary and I look forward to reminiscing about old times but just changing the subject, I have a pressing question which I need to get off my chest."

"You haven't changed one bit, you're still a worrier, ay Robbie? I can see those worry lines already forming across your forehead."

"Afraid so, that's why I thought it a good idea to touch base with an old mate who's in the police force. As you know, my uncle was a treasure hunter and you wouldn't know this but I became his sole beneficiary."

"Well lucky you, it's not something I'd be worrying over. Some people have all the luck in this life. So you want to make amends for your parents ripping us off?" taunted Colin. "I won't say no when it comes to righting a wrong. How much do you want to give me?"

"No, I think that matter was between our parents at the time, Colin, and it's time to move on. My big worry is that I know very little about my uncle's exploits and whether he has always abided by the law. In particular, I know little about who owns or gets what if a treasure is found in New Zealand waters. Like, is there tax involved? Does a portion go to the Government? And supposing the treasure was from say… the General Grant, then does the Australian Government or relatives of the descendants that may have owned the gold have legal rights? It's all such a big worry. Mary, my wife, has been telling me that I'll get a stomach ulcer."

"And she's right, but when have you ever listened to wise advice? So you think your uncle may have got his hands on the gold from the General Grant, ay? You know I wouldn't put it past him, after all he was a successful treasure hunter of world repute." Colin had put down his beer mug and sat back looking very interested. So many unsuccessful salvage operations on the General Grant had taken place over the last century.

Could Robbie's uncle have managed to accomplish what others had failed to do?

"So who was your uncle's business partner when this was supposed to have happened?" Colin asked.

"As far as I know he has had two business partners. I don't know the first one who's an Aussie but the second one is a Gregory Brown from up your way."

"Ha, you mean Sir Gregory? Now there's a controversial figure, and shady at that, if ever there was one. But these wealthy tycoons are all the same, stealing from the poor; that's how they make their money in the first place. I remember the newspaper article on him titled 'From Rags to Riches', but that just never happens unless there's some crooked dealing going on. Nobody could ever explain where all his wealth came from but if they found the gold this would explain everything." Colin leaned back in his chair. "Well I never, the gold from the General Grant."

"Anyhow, ever since I was a lad I have always suspected it, though more of a gut feeling, I'm afraid. It's just that at the funeral a man professing to have been a diver for my uncle said he wants to talk to me about the General Grant. Now, why would he say that unless my uncle had been on a salvage operation?"

"Really, why indeed?" replied Colin who looked very interested. "I think that you may be onto something and if so you can well and truly afford to make amends for your parents' shady dealing."

"What I know of the General Grant, Colin, is that it sank off the Auckland Island and at the time was carrying as much as something like five million dollars' worth of gold bars."

"Five million! No way, no way, Robbie."

"Yes, it does seem an awful lot. Do you think it was less, Colin?"

"No, it was way more than that," snorted Colin. "More like $16 million. She would have also been carrying the Steamship London's cargo of gold."

"Steamship London?"

"Yes, apparently the London was set to pick up a gold cargo from Melbourne but was lost in a storm on the way to Australia," added Colin. "Previously the London had carried about $11million of gold each trip from Melbourne to London. The General Grant would have been the only ship leaving for London at the time."

"Really, that much gold? I'm impressed. So how come you know so much about the General Grant?"

"I don't really. What I know was from a television programme screened some time ago," replied Colin. "And I'd have thought that most New Zealanders would have some knowledge about the General Grant."

"So, the London was another ship to sink in the dangerous waters of the Southern Ocean?" I asked.

"No," laughed Colin. "In fact, the London sunk in the Bay of Biscay off France and Spain."

"What?!" I exclaimed.

"I know that's surprising when many ships lost at the time were on the Australia –England route through the Southern Ocean including around the Horn. The Horn especially was notorious for shipwrecks. They called it the sailor's graveyard."

"You certainly know a lot about sailing ships, Colin," I commented.

"Thank you. Do you think your uncle may have found the treasure?"

"I don't know, Colin. Why should my uncle be successful when, for decades, others have searched and failed? The Auckland Islands are notorious for rough seas and bad weather and I'm not that sure that my uncle would be crazy enough to go there. I'm probably worrying again over nothing and seem to do that more and more these days as I get older. In all probability, thinking about it, the survivors had plenty of time marooned on the island to salvage everything of value and to hide it, then once rescued return and retrieve the bounty. That would explain why the treasure hasn't been found. They were after all stranded for eighteen months. That's an awfully long time to think about it, and recover and stash the booty."

Colin laughed, "Ha, sounds great in theory, Robbie, but these people had only the clothes on their back and were trying to survive on a remote island known for its bitterly cold, wet weather. I'm not sure they'd be keen to brave the cold unpredictable waters that had claimed many of their fellow passenger's lives, especially when survival came down to the last match. I'm sure that putting their lives at risk diving for gold would be the last thing on their minds. I'm more inclined to think your uncle found it. But that leaves you with the question of legality and something worth worrying over."

"And many sleepless nights," I added.

Colin laid down his glass. "I'm no expert, but as I understand things, treasure-hunters have salvaging rights and from a police point of view it's not like theft; it's more a case of finders keepers."

"Well, that's certainly put my mind at rest," I said.

"But," added Colin, "that doesn't rule out civil claims and I would never rule out the Tax Department."

"No, what I feared," I retorted, "and as I understand they're already sniffing around."

"Anyhow, keep me informed and in the meantime I'll discretely ask around, but I would suggest you keep this matter to yourself," advised Colin. "You may end up needing police protection if you are sitting on a haul of gold. You might very well find it difficult selling that number of gold bars especially without any authenticity certificate."

"I'm no expert on gold, but I would have thought that you could tell by the weight. Nothing has the same weight as gold does it?"

"That's not true, tungsten does," replied Colin. "There've been frauds where the gold has been drilled out from the bar and replaced with tungsten. Did your uncle own any properties in New Zealand where he may have stashed it away, assuming they salvaged the treasure?"

"Not that I know of," I replied. "My uncle spent most of his time overseas and stayed on the farm when he was in New Zealand."

"Well, keep me informed," said Colin, as I rose from my seat. "You may need my protection if your gut feeling is right."

Chapter 4

"Every man of ambition has to fight his century with its own weapons. What this century worships is wealth. The God of this century is wealth. To succeed one must have wealth. At all costs one must have wealth."
Oscar Wilde

Selected breeds of dogs serve as an integral part of New Zealand farm life. They're not only essential for rounding up the sheep and cattle but also serve as an early warning system of any visitors coming up the drive. Our Border Collie, Sam, and our Huntaway, Dynamo, were particularly vigilant at announcing the presence of any visitors well before they made it to the door. Normally Sam would commence with an excited bark then, approaching the visitor, he would press his nose into a leg, demanding affection. Dynamo would also join in the chorus with his deep bark before trying to jump up and lick the face of the visitor. Such a hospitable pair except when it came to the pastor. His arrival spelt danger; the danger of being trampled underfoot.

Unbeknown to me, Mary, who had become increasingly concerned about my anxiety, had arranged a visit from our local pastor. She thought that perhaps his intervention might help return me to a more rational state even though he did have an opinion on everything. In his own words, he was a man who knew what he was talking about as he had experienced the world, so to speak. Given his troubled background, he was not at all the typical type who entered the ministry. Miraculously he had found the Lord while serving time in prison, though he never spoke of his past deeds as this was now a closed chapter in his life which he had no desire to revisit. His Paul-like conversion accompanied by his charisma, as a big man with a deep voice, attracted many to the church, even if these new-comers were mostly odd-bods: transient fruit pickers and sorters working on orchards, farmhands, shearers and even hippies who floated around the province of Southland. But any exponential church growth has to be viewed positively, especially when it goes against national trends. Since the pastor had only been with us a short time, this growth certainly supported his continued tenure, despite those of us farm owners and businessmen — the middleclass — being less accepting of his leadership, given his dubious past. Our unchristian thoughts were "does a leopard ever change its spots?"

Following our dogs' initial barking, the pastor's four-wheeled drive noisily skidded to a stop and shortly afterwards a car door slammed shut. The shingle screamed as the big man of at least 150 kilos crunched across the shingle drive towards the house. Not only did the farm dogs give him a wide berth but the free-range hens, which had been hanging around for scraps, noisily scattered in all directions lest they too were squashed underfoot. Such was his untaught ways, he didn't bother to knock but just bowled in nosily surveying the room, before thrusting his bulging carcass onto one of the kitchen seats. It creaked under the stress but fortunately supported his weight. It didn't take long for him to spot the pots steaming over the hot plates and the roast sizzling in the oven. Dinner time was always the best time to visit parishioners, especially farmers where you always got served a good portion of meat and spuds.

"My, that roast smells so good, Mary." The pastor smacked his lips.

Mary jumped as the pot had been boiling and she hadn't heard him come in. She turned around producing a smile, "Pastor, please come in and make yourself at home. Thanks for coming at such short notice and thank you for taking Robbie's uncle's service."

"My pleasure," said the pastor leaning back on the chair.

"Excellent timing, would you like to join us for a meal?" Mary smirked, as she knew about the pastor's tendency to turn up around meal-times.

"Well, I came to have a chat with Robbie and wouldn't like to impose."

"Oh, Pastor," ribbed Mary, "you're very welcome."

"I guess bad timing on my part but mmm…that sure smells so good and I can't remember when I last had a roast. Yes, that does smell so good. If it's no trouble then I think I can certainly juggle my busy timetable around a little to fit in a meal." The pastor smacked his lips again just thinking about the roast lamb. "When it comes to cooking nobody does it better than farmers' wives," he added. He loved being a rural pastor and he had impeccable timing when it came to visiting parishioners.

"Yes," replied Mary. "We have our uses and now and again we've been known to help out on the farm."

"I would have come earlier to convey my condolences, Mary, but at the time you both seemed to be coping so well after the loss of Robbie's uncle. It's not so bad when the person had a good innings and reaches 80 or so. Their death is often a blessing; a relief from suffering. I hadn't realised that

Robbie and his uncle had been so close. Deaths I find difficult to accept are those where the person is young and in their prime. It is then I'm left to answer the question of how can a loving God do this?"

"And the answer?" asked Mary, who was now adding more water to the carrots. "What's your answer?"

"Mary, I was hoping you wouldn't ask as I'm afraid that's not an easy question." The pastor shuffled his large torso in the seat at the same time as his stomach loudly rumbled at the thought of more food. "Sometimes death is a blessing and other times it is a case of human error I guess. In others again, there's just no rational explanation, except the comfort of an afterlife. Really, I have no explanation."

I had now joined the pastor at the table after having been out moving sheep to another paddock where cows had been grazing. Unlike sheep, they don't eat the grass right down to the roots.

"Thanks for coming. My uncle's death was a blessing and I have come to terms with it. Just one matter that does trouble me a little, Pastor." I leaned back in my seat and at the same time tried to ignore the stomach sounds coming from under the table which I initially thought to be one of the dogs even though they'd been trained not to come inside.

"A little trouble, you?!" laughed Mary. "Now that's an understatement. You've been an emotional wreck, one your uncle would certainly have taken a wide berth of. Most people in your position would have been expressing gratitude rather than pessimism."

"Oh!" The pastor looked puzzled, this time producing a different sound from under the table. "Squeaky chair," explained the pastor.

"I think that the springs need oiling," replied Mary, smirking.

"Springs? It's a wooden chair, Mary," I said, unfazed by the untimely interruption. "What Mary is trying to say is that I solely inherit my uncle's estate."

"Really?" The pastor rubbed his hands gleefully. "Well if you don't want it the Lord will gladly take it off your hands. The Lord giveth and the Lord taketh. He has great plans for our community which is badly in need of financing."

"Not quite the issue," I replied sternly. "I also have pressing needs on the farm. A cash injection is well overdue. My issue lies with the source of my uncle's wealth."

"Oh!" The pastor looked perplexed. "I thought your uncle was an explorer; a treasure-hunter."

"Yes, my uncle was a treasure-hunter, but let's assume that he found a treasure like that of the General Grant, would he have been entitled to it all or would he owe the Tax Department and others?"

The pastor sat up, quite excited. "He found the treasure of the General Grant? My boy our prayers are definitely answered, halleluiah! We have so much planned for the community."

"No, I don't know that," I replied, "but it's starting to look that way. My worry is not the treasure but what problems this might bring for me if he did. Like there could be all sorts of claims: ancestors of those who owned the gold, the Australian government, the New Zealand government, the IRD. This could end up a can of worms rather than a blessing."

"A lot of ifs and buts," replied the pastor. "It does seem to me a little premature to be worrying when you've absolutely no idea at this stage. I have to agree with Mary that you are making a lot out of nothing. But keep me informed anyway. This is exciting and I'm intrigued to find out where this all goes."

"Exactly, a lot of worry over nothing. As I've told Robbie many times he's heading for a stomach ulcer." Mary put plates of food on the table and frowned in my direction. "You need to relax."

"Robbie, Jesus said, 'render to Caesar the things that are Caesar's; and to God the things that are God's'." The pastor, irreverently forgetting grace, spiked a large slice of roast lamb with his fork and shovelled it into his mouth.

"So, Robbie," said Mary, "In other words if there's tax to pay or whatever you'll just have to pay it like everyone else. That's the law and simply nothing to worry about. You'll presumably still end up with the greater portion if this treasure does exist, which I doubt very much."

"And of course you'll remember your church if you just happen to be so lucky." The pastor managed to precariously balance another huge mouthful onto his fork before sending it on its way to an excited rumbling stomach.

"I guess you're both right. I've been very silly and am getting a bit ahead of myself." I cut up some roast lamb and put this with potato on my fork.

"Red Kings," said the pastor looking at my potato. "Some of the best food in the country is down here in Southland. And the Southland swede —

delicious after weathering a good frost, now that is something to write home about especially coming from a one-eyed North Islander.”

“So what part of the North Island did you come from?” asked Mary.

“I’m a Jafa — an Auckland boy.” The pastor managed to balance the last of the food onto his fork.

“You were raised there?” I asked.

“Raised?” The pastor laughed loudly, almost losing the mouthful of food in the process. “Heaven forbid! More like abandoned and left to get into trouble. My parents were more interested in partying, smoking pot and getting drunk and sad to say both never reached an old age.” He paused and finished the food still in his mouth. “They spent the money on themselves and sent me to school most days without any lunch. These days they’d call it child poverty, whereas I’d call it irresponsible parenting.”

“That’s terrible.” Mary picked up the pastor’s plate which one could have sworn had been licked clean. She took the empty plates to the sink and began washing them down.

“So that’s when you got into trouble with the law?” I asked.

“Trouble?” The pastor laughed as he glanced over towards Mary to see if there was a dessert to follow. “I spent most of my time on the streets; Trouble was my middle name, Robbie. Believe me, before I met the Lord I was not a very nice guy.”

“Oh!” Exclaimed Mary. “Thank goodness you’ve changed. I would offer you seconds but I need to keep enough for the boys who are off playing footy and will be very hungry when they return.”

“Football! Love the game. I used to play goalie.” The pastor looked excited.

“No, no, the boys play rugby,” clarified Mary.

“Yes, so confusing these days when people talk about football. They can mean soccer, rugby, gridiron, Australian rules and goodness knows,” I added.

“Oh, and I forgot, Jack will need a meal,” Mary shuddered. “He’s so creepy and freaks me out.”

“He’s OK, dear. Just that he comes from a less fortunate life,” I replied. “Whereas we have been blessed.”

“Jack, the name sounds familiar. Do I know him?” asked the pastor.

“No, not Jack. He’s a stranger to Gore. He’s a bit of an enigma; one of these people who comes and goes between farms offering his labour in exchange for a meal and lodgings. The man arrived not long after my uncle died and he's been very useful making me new farm gates and helping me rewire some paddock fences. Our cattle can be quite hard on the gates when they're in a destructive mood or wanting to scratch their backs." I picked up a tissue and wiped my mouth and greasy hands.

"Yes, we put Jack in Robbie's grandparent's house up the drive. Before Robbie's uncle went into a home he was living there for a few months." Mary rinsed the plates before filling the electric jug.

"So then, may I ask, what's for dessert? Pavlova's my favourite." The pastor smacked his lips and his stomach rumbled in agreement. There was always room for more, especially dessert.

"Sorry, we've stopped having dessert as I became concerned about Robbie's beer-pot," Mary replied. "At one time he was slim and handsome and had an athletic body, but I guess age has caught up as it does."

"I'm a growing lad," I chipped in, patting my stomach.

"Maybe, but growing out not up," laughed Mary. "At one time we used to have pavlova pudding when we had overseas students visit and stay. It was one way of introducing them to New Zealand's famous dessert."

"Well, I guess I'll just have to settle for a coffee," hinted a disappointed pastor. "Then I really will have to be on my way. A pastor's job is never done: a funeral next week and a wedding next month, then I've still got to prepare Sunday's sermon. Overworked and underpaid, that's my job, but I'm not complaining."

The pastor downed his coffee and rose from the table. The dogs quickly retreated from the doorstep where they had been waiting in anticipation of dining on the scraps. They quickly moved to safer ground and the hens followed suit as the pastor crunched his way back to his car and drove off.

Chapter 5

"The lawyer with the suitcase can steal more money than the man with the gun."

Mario Puzo

Winter had now certainly settled in at Gore with the ground covered over in a thick layer of snow, which might sit around for several days before melting and leaving the ground soggy. The sheep were well prepared in their nice woollen coats for the cold spell but finding the grass was a problem. Harry — my oldest son, Jack, and I had been out in the paddocks forking out hay bales — our winter feed, to the sheep when I received a phone call from my uncle's solicitor inviting me to meet with him the following week at his office in Dunedin. It seemed that my uncle had certainly taken the secrecy thing to an extreme by having his solicitor in Dunedin and his accountant in Christchurch. The call triggered those feelings of anxiety which I had managed to suppress but at least now I might have answers to the questions that had been bugging me since I was a young lad. I agreed to meet even though leaving the farm at any time was always an inconvenience. Given my experiences in the past there was always something that would turn to custard in my absence like a water pipe bursting, a fence breaking or an animal escaping.

Driving through Dunedin brought back happy memories of my childhood when on many occasions our church youth group had visited New Zealand's sixth-largest city; a city founded in 1848 by the Free Church of Scotland. I fondly recalled the old churches, museum, railway station and the university, the latter taking up much of the inner city. The university had a river running right through its grounds and this was popular for initiation ceremonies. Dunedin had become known as a university city with the students occupying much of the older inner-city housing and multi-storied Halls of Residence buildings. During the university season, Dunedin was a bustling city of young people but this changed during the university vacations after students left to return to other parts of the country. At these times Dunedin seemed to lose its heart and soul becoming reduced to a ghost town. I loved this city — my favourite city — especially because of its Scottish character and old buildings. They called it the Edinburgh of the South, Dunedin being Gaelic for Edinburgh. Living much further south, in Gore, I only managed to visit it a handful of times each year.

Adding to my enjoyment was a walk through the centre of Dunedin, the Octagon. After stopping to admire the statue of Robbie Burns, and the magnificent cathedral just behind him, I turned down Stuart Street towards the railway station; a building equally magnificent, and apparently New Zealand's most photographed. How on earth they came to this conclusion remains a mystery just like the legacy, which I would very soon learn about. It was a pity I'd forgotten to bring my camera to capture such wonderful memories (and of course the railway station), though I had taken many photographs of Dunedin before. My uncle's solicitor's worked in an old multi-storey faded concrete-block building, like most of the established buildings in this area. It had large wooden framed windows that were well overdue for another repaint.

"Take a seat," instructed Tom Scott, the solicitor, who had retreated to his swivel chair behind a large well organised desk. He looked much older than when we first met; the pale, wrinkled complexion suggesting that he was, or at some time had been, a smoker. Even older but in pristine condition was his polished wooden desk.

"Kauri?"

"No, Robert, the desk is made of rimu, but it's quite old and belonged to my father who was also a solicitor. It's old just like the person sitting behind it." Tom gave a forced laugh, then pulled a file towards him. "At least I feel that way and would dearly love to retire, Robert, but I'm afraid I'll have to work on now for quite a few more years. Unfortunately, my wife did the dirty on me and left me at a very late time in our marriage. Naturally, she took half of everything, even though most of what we had comes from my practice."

"It must be hard then being on your own now and somewhat less financially placed." I looked sympathetically towards the solicitor. "I guess that there's always National Super to fall on."

"Ha, Robert, surely you're not serious? The pension is just pocket money and I'd be left destitute without a life if I were to rely on just that. Fortunately, I'm not on my own now as I have another partner, a much younger woman, but the package deal included taking on the responsibility of her mother as well which is not at all easy. These women are both demanding and cost me a fortune to keep. Seriously, I can barely make headway even on my solicitor's income. They have expensive tastes and we seem to be always dining out at the more up-market restaurants. National Super, ha, no way. The mother is one of these people who has a sense of entitlement that the world owes her a living and everything is a right, not a privilege."

"I thought that the pension wasn't too bad," I said, thinking out loud. "People I know seem to get by on it."

"It's alright for you farmers who don't have to buy your own meat and vegetables and can claim rates and mortgage interest to reduce your taxes. Anyhow you're one of the lucky ones and I'd bet you'd like to know what's in your uncle's will?" he teased as he almost passed me the file he was holding before quickly withdrawing it and placing it back on the desk.

"I gather that's why I'm here," I replied, "otherwise it was hardly worth the two-hour drive, though it's nice to meet you again."

Tom leaned back in his chair. "I can tell you now that you won't be disappointed, but sadly there's still that matter with the Tax Department."

"IRD?"

"Yes, it's all to do with probate."

"Probate?"

"Just a legal formality in winding up an estate. All debts need to be cleared first before the estate can be finalised." Tom glared at me, hesitated for a moment, then rose from his desk and walked over and closed the door to his room. "Just off the record… I didn't say this but, given your uncle's shady accountant, it wouldn't surprise me if there are unresolved issues with the IRD. It's nothing to do with me and I'm certainly not going to get involved and put my neck on the chopping block. I did warn your uncle but he had a mind of his own. He was a stubborn man."

"He was?" I had never seen him from that perspective.

"My understanding," continued the solicitor, "is that the IRD has opened up an investigation and, as the beneficiary, you may be required to attend, probably in Christchurch. Quite unprecedented but the IRD have wide powers and can do this if they think there is income that should be taxed. I've never ever come across this sort of thing before but I'm not at all surprised. His accountant is bad news, unscrupulous, and I'll leave him to explain everything."

"But don't the IRD know that my uncle is dead? How can you tax a dead man?"

"Ha! Doesn't matter one iota with the IRD. They can still tax the estate. All tax debt and any other debt must be paid first and the IRD can go back seven years or, in the case of fraud or total omission, any number of years, and on any amount they consider to be owing. Then there is the use of money interest and short-fall penalties. Imagine interest on interest and debt over many years."

"That could be financially crippling," I replied.

"Exactly, Robert, and it has been in the past for some who thought they could get away with not declaring all their income. Many years may pass by and one may think they are scot-free then wham, an IRD audit. But that's not my problem and I refuse to be involved." Tom, who had now gone a shade of pink, picked up a glass and gulped a mouthful of water. It was more-so to calm his nerves. "Anyhow, regardless, there's no need to worry, you're still going to be a wealthy man as you're the only beneficiary coming from a one-child family and a childless uncle. Pity your uncle hadn't thought of including me in his will as an appreciation for all the help I've given him over the years. I've sorted out many difficult problems for him and that's the thanks I get." The lawyer sighed. "At this stage of life, given my circumstances, it would have helped me immensely in my retirement." Tom slowly drew the file towards him and opened it then tapped his fingers on the table. "Wait for it, your uncle has left you the grand sum of ...$931,259, less of course, any further solicitor and accountant's fees. I guess that was far more than you ever anticipated?"

"Well, no, I don't want to seem ungrateful, but I thought my uncle's adventures had netted him millions. "The General Grant alone would have…"

"General Grant, General Grant?" Tom looked up, quite perplexed. "I thought that this wreck was still lying on the seafloor somewhere south of Stewart Island. I recall from newspaper reports attempted salvage operations in 1986 and 1996 by a Bill Day. From memory, his party entered the cave where the boat sank and carried out a thorough search of the seabed. I think he had something like eleven divers and they searched the cave bottom with a tooth comb removing rocks and boulders in the process. Oh, but then again he found nothing."

"Amazing, that you can come up with the actual years and facts," I said. To think somebody could out of the blue recall facts just from reading a newspaper decades later was unbelievable.

"Not so amazing. I'm a lawyer, Robert," laughed Tom. "When we do all our law examinations we have to remember cases, facts and their years. We have to have an exceptional memory for years and facts. But on recollection, I have to admit I did get something wrong. The first Day expedition didn't come away with nothing. On the first occasion, they found an anchor and even part of a cannon and on the second expedition, after they had cleared the bottom of boulders and other rubble, found some silver and gold coins and a surgeon's kit."

"So then they found the General Grant?" I looked disappointed.

"No, it wasn't the General Grant," replied Tom. "The coins all well and truly predated the General Grant and all the artefacts recovered suggested that the wreckage was of a ship lost around 1833. Records showed that the only ship to sail from Australia between 1830 and 1834 that went missing was a trading vessel called the Rifleman and one of the passengers was a surgeon, thus accounting for the surgeon's kit."

"Let me get this straight. This ship came to grief in the same cave but prior to the General Grant and all they found was what remained of the Rifleman?"

"Correct," Tom replied.

"So, if the General Grant's treasure was there then it would have been buried on top of what they found," I said.

"Well yes, you're totally right. It would have to be wouldn't it?" Tom now looked quite perplexed.

"Then it's conceivable that if the treasure was not there then it had already been removed and just maybe that's because my uncle found the gold from the wreckage long before Bill Day."

"The General Grant, are you sure? I know your uncle was into finding shipwrecks but he never mentioned to me about salvaging the General Grant and, to date, I've heard nothing publicly of the treasure being recovered. Your uncle was always very secretive and he kept me in the dark when it came to his adventures though. Well, I'd be; the crafty devil, and he kept this quiet all these years though he was required by law to disclose a successful salvage. Yes, that could very well explain the IRD's involvement as the recovered treasure is income in their eyes. But if you're right then what happened to this treasure as his estate would certainly be worth much more, as you say? I can tell you that your uncle has had a lot of money in the past but over the last decade it was quickly depleted given his lifestyle and love of cruise ships. He thought that in his frail state that the best alternative by far to living in a rest home was to live on cruise ships."

"Yes, he told us that many times," I replied. "He always argued that there was little difference in the annual cost of the passage on a cruise ship to living in a Rest Home, and the cruise ship came with a doctor, room service, as well as exceptionally better food, entertainment and adventure. A Rest Home was, in the end, the death of him. Still, I'm sure even over a decade he wouldn't have spent much more than half a million."

"Oh, I don't know about that." Tom hesitated as if lost in thought. "The General Grant, well I'll be." He nervously fidgeted for a moment, then reluctantly reached into his top drawer, producing an envelope.

"Here," he said, slowly sliding the envelope in my direction. "Probably nothing but your uncle also wanted you to have this. I think it's a key but to what I don't know. If it's a property or something of value then I will need to include it in the estate assets, otherwise, I know nothing about this envelope and don't want to know if it's of a dubious nature, OK?"

"If it's the General Grant's gold?" I asked.

"Then I most certainly need to know," replied the solicitor, sitting upright in his chair. "I don't want to see you getting into trouble. It would certainly open up a can of worms but maybe we can work out something to avoid involving the authorities."

"OK," I replied, as I tucked the envelope securely into my pocket, placing a handkerchief on top. Maybe this was a key to a hidden cellar; an Aladdin's cave, where gold from the General Grant, and diamonds, rubies, sapphires and other precious items from other wrecks, had been stored.

"Oh, before I forget," added Tom, "your uncle wanted to add conditions to your inheritance as he felt you needed to stretch your legs out on an adventure or two and take a break from the farm. My reply was that the more complex you make a will, the more contestable it'll be. The best wills are simple like the shortest ever will, 'All to Mother'."

"So what was it he wanted?" I asked, as I reluctantly returned to my seat, cringing at the thought that solicitors charge for their time.

"Best that I answer this with a story about your uncle's early adventures." Tom leaned back in his chair and gulped another mouthful of water and I surreptitiously checked the time on my watch.

"Many years ago your uncle began his adventures by teaming up with an Australian by the name of Wally Devine."

"Wally? Yes, I recall Uncle in conversations mentioning that name when I was little."

"To continue, Wally owned a boat and he, his girlfriend, Martha, and your uncle sailed the world in search of wrecks with treasures. As I understand it Martha was an Australian girl and very attractive and she often spent the time sunbathing on deck in a bikini while Wally was diving. Your uncle didn't dive much and also spent much time on deck while Wally was searching the ocean bed. I think you can conclude where this is going already. Anyway, there was an incident which your uncle would not share about but I suspect some sort of foul play involving other actors. Anyhow, whatever it was your uncle was very scared and wanted out. On top of this Martha also wanted to leave Wally and distance herself from this situation. She pressed your uncle to join her. While Wally was asleep downstairs in the cabin they abandoned him and the ship. Unbeknown to your uncle, she had commandeered the spoils retrieved from Wally's dive and not long after they made dry land she dumped your uncle."

"Oh, how terrible!" I was shaken. This was not like the uncle I had believed to be celibate.

"Your uncle always felt bad about abandoning Wally in this way, especially running off with his girlfriend. He was hoping that you could visit Wally in Denpasar and explain how he'd been played by Martha."

"Denpasar? Where on earth on this planet is Denpasar?"

"Bali, Robert. Well, what do you say? If you decide not to then you'll still get the inheritance regardless but this was important to your uncle and was a death-bed wish."

"You mean he wants me to face up to a hostile reception in Bali, Tom? Sending the lamb to the slaughter."

"More so the shepherd in this case," Tom laughed. "Take the break. Bali is beautiful. It will do you and your wife the world of good and I'm sure an 80-year-old man — even still angry today, won't be any threat. If anything it may heal a few wounds and who knows, Wally may be able to fill in the gaps and lead you to more of your uncle's treasure if it exists. Of course, if you find more keep me posted."

My mind raced ahead. Perhaps there could be something in taking a trip to Bali, a break from farming sheep. I was eager to learn more about my uncle. Who was he really, and what were his secrets? I'm sure that Wally might be a wealth of knowledge and willing to part with secrets now as an 80-year-old, or did he too intend to take them to his grave?

Yes," I replied, "a trip to Bali could be quite entertaining and I'm sure Mary would welcome a shopping opportunity. I understand it's very cheap there and there are lots of lovely beaches."

"You and Mary will have to get a massage," laughed the solicitor. "Very cheap and most relaxing. Do you surf?"

"No."

"A pity, Robert."

I left the solicitor a little bit wiser to my inheritance and somewhat eager to open the envelope. Perhaps here may lie the answers to the General Grant.

Chapter 6

"Three may keep a secret, if two of them are dead."

Benjamin Franklin

"Well?" asked Colin. "The million-dollar question, did he leave you the gold?" Colin picked up his glass of beer and took a mouthful, waiting impatiently for my response. I sat back in the metal-framed seat and stared over towards the bar. For this time on a Friday evening, I thought that Traffers looked rather empty. Perhaps the township had taken off to Dunedin for the super-rugby clash between the Highlanders and the Crusaders. This was always going to be a well-contested game when the Crusaders from Canterbury came south.

"Gold?" I repeated as I planned my response which was aimed at not giving too much away.

"Yes, gold. Well?" repeated Colin impatiently.

"No such luck." I emptied the jug of beer into my glass. "I have no idea about the General Grant. My uncle's involvement, if any, remains a mystery and it seems that the more corners I turn, the more questions than answers I get. I thought that I knew my uncle but I guess I was wrong. I wish he had shared his secrets before he went to the grave."

"So you're telling me that a successful treasure-hunter left you, the only heir, just a pittance? I don't believe it, Robbie. Even at his funeral, a number of speakers alluded to his fame and great fortune. Your uncle was rolling in money, especially after finding the pirate's treasure."

"Oh no! I wouldn't say that at all, Colin. The amount is much less than what I would have expected especially if his exploits had included the General Grant's treasure."

"Do you mind me asking how much?" Colin asked.

"Less than a million," I replied, "but I'm hoping that the key might hold some clues, and maybe there's more to come," I added.

"Key!" Colin let the glass of beer slip from his grasp onto the pub table with a thud. "What key?" I now had Colin's full attention.

I hesitated as I hadn't planned on telling Colin about the key and I felt like kicking myself for letting it slip. At times it seemed that I couldn't help myself and wanted to disclose everything. I guess that it was an inescapable part of my personality.

"The inheritance included an envelope in which I found a key. A note from my uncle accompanied it telling me that this is to a safety deposit box in an Auckland bank of all places. My uncle did, for some reason, want to scatter his accountant, solicitor and everything else around the country."

"Storage shed more likely," Colin sniggered. "Not a pittance then, sure? The fact is that you're going to be filthy rich. So when are you shooting up to Auckland then?"

"I'm keen to fly up to Auckland in the near future, Colin, but in case you forgot, I do have a farm to run and there's a mountain of work to be done. You've lived on a farm and will know that it's never-ending."

"One thing's for sure." Colin picked up his empty jug. "You can certainly afford to shout this poor policeman another beer. Some of us don't get the same breaks in life and work hard for a pittance. Then, what we do have, the government and banks steal away from us. It is not a fair world."

"Of course I can buy a mate a beer or even two," I agreed. "It looks like I may have to find time around all the farm work to also visit Christchurch soon. Goodness knows what my uncle and his accountant have done to upset the IRD."

"Might I suggest the General Grant, perhaps? Oh, haha, the old IRD. The best of luck Robbie, my lad," laughed Colin, as he took another mouthful of beer. "You know, in America, it was the IRS, not the cops, who nailed Al Capone. It's not so easy for us cops as we need warrants and anything we do comes under public scrutiny. Then, when we do arrest someone, these soft judges let them out on a good behaviour bond, meaning we have to waste our precious time finding and arresting them all over again when they fail to turn up in court. Ludicrous! Tell me where do they find these nutters who design such time-wasting systems? Now the tax department, that's a different story. They have a different set of rules and far wider powers. Be warned, they can walk right into your house and walk out with your computer or any other records relating to your business and they don't have to go to a judge first for a warrant."

"No trouble there," I replied. "My business is squeaky clean. I've even accounted for the number of beasts I've taken for the family dinner plate. If they sniff around all they'll find are the sheep dags, for what they're worth."

"But maybe the same can't be said about your uncle," warned Colin. "Perhaps I can do a mate's favour and collect the contents of your deposit box for you as I'm going up to Auckland next week. I have to turn up as a police witness in court for a case I worked on. To think that I'd left the big smoke for good. No such luck."

"Tut tut, Colin, that would be like asking somebody to open my Christmas presents. No, I'm looking forward to the surprise, though I anticipate some boring private notes, maybe some obscure treasure maps. Treasure-hunting is certainly not my thing, especially when there's a stack of jobs on the farm that need to be done before shearing and lambing kick in. With this bad weather: snow, sleet and rain, it's hard enough finding a good day to get anything done."

"Treasure maps?" Colin's eyes lit up. "If you don't want them then I'll gladly take them off your hands. Hunting for treasure sounds exciting."

"No, I have two sons, one at least who would be very interested," I replied. "You know it's quite peculiar, but at the time I had a feeling that the solicitor was somewhat reluctant to pass me that key. It was odd that he had it tucked away in his top drawer rather than being with my uncle's file on the desk."

"Oh! Now that sounds rather dodgy, but Robbie, they're all like that. I hope for your sake that you didn't tell him about the General Grant?"

"I did, but he seemed to know nothing about it and wanted to know more."

"Robbie, Robbie, of course, he wanted to know more! Never ever trust solicitors especially after what they did to my parents."

"Divorce can be very messy," I replied. "It's unfortunate that your parents had to go through it."

"And barristers," added Colin. "Some of these same legal firms also do barrister work and represent some of the most hardened criminals in our society. They mix with these people, maybe on more than a professional basis and could even be in league if it's lucrative."

"Hm, I guess you have a point, Colin. Greed is rampant in our society, but it's not just solicitors and barristers."

"Do you trust politicians, Robbie?"

"No of course not, Colin. Who does? They make election promises that they seldom keep and they nearly always try to weasel out of telling the truth when they're shoulder deep into a hole. Talk about the absence of accountability. Please don't get me started, Colin. The number of times they've let down the farmers in New Zealand are more than I can remember and now they're trying to blame farmers for pollution and global warming. What cows do is just part of the carbon dioxide cycle. Through photosynthesis, the grass absorbs carbon dioxide from the air and grows, and the cows eat the grass and poo. This breaks down into the soil and the carbon dioxide then returns to the air to go through the same cycle. You don't have to be a brain surgeon to understand that."

"Exactly," Colin put down his glass. "And you're aware that many politicians were solicitors or barristers first?"

"No, I wasn't but, come to think about it, I think you're right."

"I make my point. You can't trust any of them, and they're so expensive. Once the bank had grabbed their share of my parents' property in money owing, the solicitors came in and grabbed another large chunk. They'd charge you for the air you breathe in their office if they could. Now tell me how many people have you told about the General Grant? Believe me, when you work the small hours of the night you get to see the other half of society, the not so nice people: drunks, druggies, prostitutes, thugs and hard-core criminals. You only need to tell one or two people and they tell one or two, then sooner or later it reaches the criminal world and before you know it your house will be ransacked or worse. I've seen it happen before, so tell no one, Robbie. I'm serious."

"Colin, you sound like my uncle and look at the legacy of unanswered questions he left behind. This is Gore, a peaceful little town of law-abiding people. When you work in a city of two million like Auckland you can expect to see all sorts, but not here in Gore. We're all good people here. Besides, I took your advice and I've only told the family, the solicitor and pastor. I didn't tell Jack or any of the neighbours."

"Who's Jack?"

"Oh, just a nice bloke who turned up one day looking for work. But it probably wouldn't matter if I had told him; he's just a homeless soul content to have a meal and bed for the night."

"Did you do a police check on him first and did he supply you with references?"

"No, Colin."

"Then what do you know about him, Robbie?"

"Absolutely nothing except that the poor man needed food and lodgings. We had an empty cottage, and Mary and I have been so blessed with the farm. The least we can do is to help this poor soul get back onto his feet."

"Oh, dear! So you think then that the criminal element stops south of the Bombay Hills, ay Robbie? Is that what you're saying? Believe me, we're no different from any other country in the world. Organised crime stretches far and wide to all four corners of New Zealand. Bikie gangs have carved New Zealand into territories and hard-core criminals are engaged in illegal activities throughout the country. There's another world out there most law-abiding people never get to see unless they fall victim."

"Well, not that many people know about my uncle and the General Grant, and I'm still not sure if it's even true. Apart from the diver in Auckland, nobody seems to know anything or that's what they tell me. I guess all might be revealed when I get to open the safety deposit box. I think I'll try to kill two birds with one stone and see if I can touch base with this diver as well when I'm next in Auckland. The diver seems to have all the answers."

"Good. That'll be a long drive," joked Colin.

"No driving intended," I replied. "These days at my age I'd be lucky if I was able to manage two days each way driving. Then there's the horrendous cost of taking a vehicle on the ferry across Cook Strait."

"Yes, the ferry cost over the years has been a good excuse for North Islanders not travelling south and South Islanders not travelling north. Ferry and petrol-wise it's probably cheaper these days flying for a holiday to Australia."

"Well, I'll be flying to Auckland," I said, before draining the remaining beer from my glass. "I haven't the time to waste driving."

"You can hire a car from the airport, anyhow." Colin likewise emptied his glass. "You'll find that the motorways are pretty good now for getting you to wherever you want to go to in Auckland."

"No, not this country lad, Colin. I'd be lost in the Auckland traffic and I'm not brave enough to tackle that motorway. This country lad is used to driving on single-lane highways and narrow shingle back-roads. I think I'd freak out having to jump lanes in the big smoke and on deciding which out of three or four lanes I need to take to avoid ending up in Whangarei or Hamilton. No, it will have to be taxis and buses for me this time, I'm afraid."

Chapter 7

"Don't trust everything you see…Even salt looks like sugar."

Maryum Ahsam

Jack was putting up a gate he had built when I joined him. Perhaps Colin was right about Jack and I should've checked him out first, but it wasn't as if I was employing him. Police checks also take time and Jack is hardly likely to wait around to be cleared when meanwhile he can find another farm that will take him in without any fuss.

Mary had also suggested that I was crazy employing someone I didn't know who miraculously one day appeared on our doorstep shortly after it had become public knowledge that I was to inherit my uncle's estate. She was, as usual, right as he might have a criminal record, be on the run from the law or canvassing the neighbourhood for future criminal activities, or he might even be a treasure-hunter keen on learning from me where my uncle had been exploring in hope that he might also find treasure. But on the latter I had few worries because I had little to offer, as my uncle was tight-lipped when it came to sharing his adventures. Mary now felt nervous about walking alone around the farm even down the drive to feed the hens lest she bumped into Jack. He could, for all we know, be a convicted rapist. It seemed that these days murderers and rapists seemed to spend hardly any time in prison before being released back into the community. They could be circulating amongst us without us ever knowing about their horrendous crimes. I guess for a short woman any tall strongly-built male stranger in close proximity in a private rural setting could be perceived as intimidating. However, as a Christian, I had a heart for the poor and homeless and welcomed the opportunity to provide him with food and lodging. It was not for me to judge another and one cannot dismiss a stranger based solely on their unkempt appearance and rough speech.

It was true that his appearance was not at all becoming with his long greasy hair and a moth-eaten cotton-brush shirt that he had worn over the last five days (at least it smelt that way). Added to this were his dirty stained shorts, and well-worn work boots that had seen better days. He was, by his dishevelled appearance, a man who was destitute and in need of a friend, yet an enigma given his impressive skills and knowledge. Perhaps at one time in his life, he'd been a farmer or skilled farmhand. Maybe he had experienced a crisis in life: a mental break-down, divorce, bankruptcy or something else. It wasn't for me to judge, and having a volunteer on the farm was an added bonus, especially at a time between the infrequent paycheques for lamb, calf and wool sales. Farming wasn't like a townie job where you receive a fortnightly paycheque. As farmers, we were very much dependent on supply and demand and the amount we'd eventually receive from sales. We were in no great position to pay out weekly wages without borrowing from the bank, something we tried to avoid. What we could do ourselves we did; especially the shearing because these days there would otherwise be no profit after paying shearers' wages.

To think that people like Jack just wandered the countryside picking up some work here and other work there and were content to just have a full stomach and a night's lodgings was a mystery. Most people, I'd have thought, would also want a bit of money to occasionally spoil themselves. Perhaps this was just my own narrow middle-class perception, my world view. Jack had asked if he could set possum traps on the farm and I was more than happy for him to rid my farm of this pest and any others like weasels, stoats and rabbits. If he wanted to catch them and skin them then he was most welcome to what money he could make from their sale. I had my doubts though, believing that the possum catches would be small in number and would not bring him much in the way of income. He also collected pinecones for sale which I was also happy about as they were otherwise just rotting on the ground. If there was money in it for him then good luck. Maybe he was also drawing the dole, which would explain how he was able to maintain and run his car. Jack was not unlike others in the larger neighbourhood and further afield, who were transient and happy to trudge through life working for next to nothing on farms and orchards for a short period before disappearing into thin air from whence they'd come.

"Well, where will you go after you're finished with this farm?"

Jack continued to work away and initially, I thought that this was another occasion where he was not going to reply. Like my uncle, he had selective hearing and parted with little information. I had not learned any more about him since the day he arrived on our door-step.

"There are other farms," he muttered, as he slid the gate into position. "The bulls won't be able to knock this one over with their bums," he added, referring to the new gate. "This one's solid as and I daresay that your bulls would be well and truly off for the chop before they get to be a handful."

"Thanks, a professional job," I replied, extremely pleased as I closed the gate. "Well, I guess we can get on with the fencing. That wind gust last night snapped off a tree branch taking out several metres of fence. Fencing seems to be never-ending, given wind and cattle."

"Sure," Jack grunted as he picked up his tools — well actually my tools. Then we walked over to the tractor. This would save a long walk to the offending fence-line. "I told ya what you needed to do though about the cattle. Ya run an electric wire along the fence top that'll keep them away from the fence. A few good electric shocks up their backside, that's all they need to get the message." Jack laughed, exposing his missing incisors then turned to me.

"There's talk in the pub that ya uncle found the gold of the General Grant?"

"Sorry, the General Grant?" Jack's question had caught me off-guard.

"Ya know, that old sailing boat that sank down South and all that gold," said Jack. "I hear it must've been millions of dollars."

"Well, yes, it's true that my uncle was a treasure-hunter and dived for sunken wrecks but I can't see how he would've been successful in this case when many others have failed to find the wreck," I replied. "Who's been spreading this wild rumour?"

Jack leapt up onto the tractor. "Dun know, the guys I was drinking with. Just current pub gossip that's all bro. So ya says it's not true?"

"I wish it was," I replied, as I started up the tractor. "It would be nice to have all that gold. There's a lot of things that need doing on the farm, if I only had the money."

"Ya uncle lived on the farm, so I hear?"

"Yes, the few times when he was in New Zealand," I shouted above the clamour of the motor. "In fact, he lived in your house."

Jack nodded and I couldn't make out his response over the tractor motor as at times he tended to mumble. He looked satisfied with my response.

As the day passed I became more and more concerned that perhaps I had become too generous in information sharing and it seemed to be one-way when it came to Jack. He seemed to ask a lot of questions and now knew an awful lot about me and my family and our business operation but we knew practically nothing about him. Was he married and did he have kids? What area of New Zealand was he raised in and why did he choose to work in this area? A man with his skills, and with a tidied-up appearance, would have no trouble picking up well-paid farm work. Jack was also tight-lipped on his politics and worldview, something odd these days when everyone seems to have an opinion on most things. It was clear though, that he had no time for religion and meeting our pastor.

I felt guilty as I walked into Traffers to join Colin for a beer or two as I had now shared about the General Grant with another person. I was pleased though, that the day had ended up being very productive as we not only had repaired the damaged fence but also the fence between two paddocks. This would certainly enhance productivity, confining the sheep and cattle to one paddock and allowing the other to regenerate. That was what was supposed to happen on a farm instead of the sheep finding gaps and spreading out into other paddocks. I was hoping Jack might stay on for at least a couple more months which would certainly be a huge step towards getting to the bottom of my farm 'to do' list. Some gates and fences needed replacing and we were quickly heading towards lambing, calving, mustering, drenching, crutching and more. Spring is one of our busiest times with sheep and cattle.

Colin looked up at me as I joined him at the table with a couple of jugs of beer in my hand. He was not happy when I told him about my conversation with Jack.

"So how do you feel about telling a man you don't know that you may have gold from the General Grant?" he scoffed. "As I said, the criminal element stretches from Cape Reinga to Bluff. I did some checking yesterday and your man, Jack, has spent time in prison."

"Really?" My jaw dropped, and I almost let the glass of beer slip from my grip onto the table at the thought that I had shared an awful lot of personal stuff about our farm and our family with Jack. "What on earth for?"

"Robbery," replied Colin. "I thought I'd do a bit of investigating as it's all easily accessible on our computers. And that's not all, your pastor has a criminal record as well."

"A lot of people have made mistakes during their lives, Colin. My pastor has been very open about his criminal past."

"Well, in his case it wasn't simply the result of one too many drinks. He has a long history of offending; a real bad one, in boots and all with organised crime."

"So, do you mind me asking what he did, Colin?"

"Armed robbery, assault, automobile theft, shop-lifting and the list goes on from a very early age. He is one to be wary of," Colin whispered, so he was not overheard by the people on the next table.

"OK, so he was once bad but now he's repented and is a new man; in fact a good Christian at that, and just maybe Jack has also turned over a new leaf as well. People do change you know, and Jack's such a good, skilled worker. Unless I catch him up to no good he's most welcome at my house anytime. The poor man is homeless and we can't condemn him for mistakes he may have made in the past. We're all sinners."

"No, Robbie. Once bad… always bad." Colin filled up his glass.

"Well, Paul changed," I retorted.

"Paul who?" asked Colin.

"Paul in the bible. He went around having Christians killed until one day he was miraculously converted. He was largely instrumental in setting up the first churches and writing at least eight books of the bible."

"Paul? The bible? Robbie, I'm surprised that you, a reasonably intelligent man, would believe all that garbage."

"Well, take somebody more recent like John Newton who wrote the song Amazing Grace. He was a slave trader in the eighteenth century who had a miraculous life-saving experience at sea. It was enough to change him from being a ruthless slave trader to becoming a pastor and fighting for the abolition of slavery. I strongly believe that our pastor is like John and is now a new man with a heart for the Lord. Perhaps Jack has changed as well."

"I think we'll have to beg to differ on this." Colin emptied his glass. "And you can keep your religion. It didn't help my parents."

Chapter 8

"Whoever has the gold makes the rules."

Anonymous

Quite unexpectedly one afternoon, a white, late model Mercedes pulled up our drive. As usual the excited barking of our dogs, Sam and Dynamo alerted us to the fact that we had a visitor. Fortunately, I had just returned from the paddocks and was there to greet our visitor, Gregory Brown (my uncle's business partner), as he stepped out of his car.

"Well, I did promise you a visit," said a slightly embarrassed Gregory. He shook my hand and at the same time pushed away our collie, Sam, who was embarrassingly pressing his nose into more private areas. "I certainly hope that this is a good time to stop by. I've come down from Auckland for a business deal in Invercargill. My wife has never been this far south before and has accompanied me."

"Your wife?" I stooped down and looked into the car.

"Oh, she's not with me I'm afraid to say. She preferred to stay in Invercargill and would sooner enjoy the comfort of a warm bed than brave a frosty start to the day. Frosts are something we're foreign to up in Auckland and that southerly wind you have down here is a bone-chiller."

"One gets used to it," I replied.

"I hope you don't mind me asking, but how did you get on with your uncle's solicitor, all those millions of dollars?" Gregory gave a forced laugh and it was hard to know whether he was just joking or deadly serious. "You know there's little point putting it in a bank where they pay a pittance in interest. I have just the investment for you and could get you a very good return."

"Millions? I wish," I responded. "Successful as my uncle may have been, not even one million in the pot, but it was a tidy and useful sum." We walked towards the house. "Thank you for your kind offer but I can see the inheritance quite quickly disappearing into farm costs."

"He left less than a million? No! That's very hard to believe. I know that your uncle would have eaten through his savings living on cruise ships over the last decade or so and of course funding treasure expeditions but I would've thought you'd still be left with a tidy seven-figure sum." Gregory looked quite shocked. "Your uncle was in many ways quite frugal, he never gambled, smoked and seldom drank. I can't believe it."

We walked inside and I introduced Gregory to my wife who was in the kitchen doing some baking.

"Nice to meet you. I was just making a cuppa." Mary walked across the room and shook Gregory's hand. "Would you like tea or coffee or something else to drink?" Mary returned to the boiling electric jug.

"Coffee will be just fine with milk and one sugar," said Gregory, as he took a seat at the kitchen table. "These days I've become quite addicted to caffeine and need my daily fix or I get a headache. It was a habit I developed when attending boring Board of Director's meetings. The coffee stopped me from drifting off. It tends to happen as you get older."

"I've heard that coffee saves the day," I quipped.

"I like the Mercedes," commented Mary, who had been looking out the window. "You can leave it here if you like."

"Yes, I bought it this year," said Gregory. "I like to replace my car with a new one every couple of years."

"Just be careful around Gore. We have a policeman who loves to give speeding tickets to people with posh cars," Mary sniggered.

"Oh, and who's that?" I asked.

"Colin, of course," replied Mary.

"Oh, Colin, that doesn't surprise me." I took another sip of my coffee.

"Well, finally I've made it as I promised your uncle I would, though sadly not when your uncle was alive. Many years ago I told him that one day I'd drop in at the farm, but life at times gets very busy and he was hardly ever around; always off gallivanting around the world."

"Tell me about it," Mary said, as she passed Gregory a coffee and surreptitiously removed my dirty lunch plate from the table. "I'm always kept busy cleaning up after Robbie; it's a full-time occupation."

"In particular," continued Gregory, smirking at Mary's comment and at my shade of pink at having been reprimanded, "I wanted to see the farm, firstly because my grandson wants me to buy one on the outskirts of Auckland and secondly because I've heard so much about your farm from your uncle."

"No problem, I'd love to give you a guided tour after we finish our drinks. I'm pleased you asked as it's not often that townies express an interest in farms. I was of the opinion that most think there's not much involved in farming other than sheep, more sheep, a herd of cows and lots and lots of grass," I laughed. "I think many believe that farmers lead a cushy life just now and again having to put down the novel to get up and rotate the sheep or give them an overdue hair-cut. You know, the sheep and cows just look after themselves."

"Well, as a townie I must plead guilty to not knowing much about farming," laughed Gregory. "I have no idea what's involved."

"I'm pleased, Gregory, that your grandson's interested in farming," I continued. "But I hope he's well aware that it's a different job to the nine to five job, five days a week that you townies are used to. Otherwise, it will be an awful shock when he buys a farm. Farming is a seven day a week job which can start in the early hours and go well past dusk. None of this forty-hour week rubbish. It's full-on days and even some nights and it's a science. For instance, we need to test the soil and attend to it like adding lime now and again and when it comes to sowing new grass it's not just any grass will do. Here in Southland most of us use a perennial ryegrass, a grass that suits our climate."

"He probably isn't aware and really neither was I, but that's no problem as he doesn't intend farming the land."

"Oh!" I put down my cup and looked shocked. "He doesn't? I thought you said…"

"He takes after his grandfather and is more interested in the bigger money. In this case the profit he can make from property development. Auckland is expanding and eventually, the surrounding farmland will be rezoned. Too long for me to wait for at my age and I don't currently have millions of dollars on hand to reinvest and have tied up. I think he'll just have to dream or find another backer. Besides I'm told that property development, while it can be lucrative, can also backfire and end up financially crippling. One needs to factor in all the hidden costs like the land you can't sell that will be required for roads and reserves, and the unexpected council fees and contractor price hikes. Then, heaven forbid, if while excavating the area you find it was a Maori burial site or once a Maori settlement, then you're sunk." Gregory sipped his coffee and took advantage of Mary's baking on offer. "One needs to do thorough research on the land's history before buying."

"Well, you won't find me selling up my land for a profit should Gore want to expand in my direction," I said. "The Government and local authorities should curtail urban sprawl and just settle for more high-rise apartments and smaller residential sections."

"Yes, there's certainly money to be made in the construction of apartments," commented Gregory rubbing his hands. "I have recently been looking into that area."

"That's not my point, Geoffrey. Politicians seem to forget that something like 40% of our export earnings come from dairying and meat and I guess about 50% if you add timber. What the farming community contributes is the difference between New Zealand being a developed or a Third World country, and every time they take more of our land for housing it makes it just a little bit harder for us to contribute to export earnings. These days farming isn't anywhere near as profitable as it has been and there's now no money in wool sales but the sheep still have to be shorn. By the time you've paid the shearers, there's just nothing left for the farmer. That's why on our farm we shear our own sheep."

"So it's true then that a farmer is a man outstanding in his field?" laughed Gregory.

"It's a case of having to be to make ends meet," I replied. "We have to be a jack of all trades."

"And a master of none," added Mary, looking at me crossly. "That pipe you said you'd fixed weeks ago is still leaking and now I have to take the long route to the veggie garden. Can you deal with it, Robbie?"

I rose from the table.

"No, you don't need to fix it right now," Mary laughed.

"I'm not," I replied. "I'm about to commence a tour and I'm sure by the time I'm finished that Gregory here will never want to see another sheep or paddock. Come, I'll take you in the ute unless you want to stretch your legs."

"So, what sort of business do you do, Gregory, if you're no longer into treasure-hunting?" I asked as we walked to the ute.

"Yes, Robbie, treasure-hunting has long passed. Those days sleeping in a poky boat cabin and eating dehydrated food have gone. I've even gone off diving as I no longer have the tolerance for icy water. These days I prefer flying business class and staying in five-star hotels. I have many different business interests, including directorships on a number of company boards, but my main activity is my asset-stripping company."

"Asset stripping?"

"Yes. I look for companies that have market share values below what their assets are worth. For instance, the share value might be $6 and the asset value $10, so I make an offer to shareholders somewhere in-between and buy up the company for a song."

"Why would anyone be silly enough to want to sell you the shares for a small profit, Gregory?"

"Greed, my boy; that's how the world operates these days. Investors have an interest in getting a good return on their investment and in this economy where annual interest rates are about 2%, anything above this is a very good tax-free return," Gregory laughed. "Then once I take ownership I strip the company, selling off its land and buildings, equipment and anything else worth money and make a handsome profit."

"But what about the employees who will be out of a job? Some will have families and mortgages and are dependent on that income."

"Tough, then they'd better start looking for another job," laughed Gregory. "That's life, it was probably their fault in the first place that the business was underperforming. We all have choices in life and too bad if someone makes a bad one and works for a failing business. I also do very well on the speculation side."

"Speculation?"

"Yes, I frequently mix with other business leaders over a beer or two and often the conversation hinges around their company performances, gossip about other companies, takeovers and other things. There's always a bob to be made buying in or selling shares before this news becomes public. There's money to be made getting in early before share prices rise."

"I thought that insider trading was illegal, Gregory"

"Oh, it is these days if you're on the Board of Directors for that company or involved in some way. I just perchance happen to get wind of what might be going to happen now and again in another company and I'm free to take a flutter. There's nothing illegal here. It's a case of who you know in this world and how much money you have to play around with," Gregory laughed. "Changing the subject, can you also show me where your uncle lived when he was on the farm? Just a matter of curiosity on my part. He often spoke of the cottage being over a hundred years old."

"Sure, it is very old and belonged to my grandparents. Since my uncle died it's been vacant but now we have Jack, a farmhand, living in there."

"I guess then that I won't be able to look inside, but that's fine. Just seeing it will satisfy my curiosity." Gregory stepped into the ute and I took him first to see my uncle's cottage.

"How long is Jack staying for?" asked Gregory.

"Jack could be here today and gone tomorrow," I replied. "He wanders from job to job wherever the wind takes him."

"Certainly not the type of person I'd employ but I guess that farming is different to my type of work," said Gregory.

We continued to drive around the farm, passing the shearing shed, barn, lake and a few paddocks before returning to the house.

"As you can see my uncle's money will soon disappear. There is so much that needs to be done and I need a new tractor, new roof on the barn, new shearing equipment and the costs just keep mounting as assets wear out."

"Quite an operation," Gregory replied. "And it certainly steers me away from investing in a farm. I don't want to be rude but there are certainly much less stressful ways of making money, especially with all that capital locked away in land and equipment. It is just not my thing. Money needs to be fluid and turned over quickly if you want to make more."

"I'm sure you're right," I replied. "But for me, it's all about lifestyle and less about percentage return. I love the country, the freedom and the wide spaces and in the end, you can't take it with you."

"Unfortunately, so true." Gregory nodded. "And one needs to enjoy it as one's children will have no qualms about living the high life off any inheritance," he added.

He did not mention the General Grant, so I didn't ask and anyhow I had the bank key and the diver in Auckland who I was sure would provide all the answers.

Chapter 9

"People who think you could wave a magic wand and the legacy of the past will be over are blind."

Ruth Bader Ginsburg

Ever since the solicitor had given me the key I had carried it around in my pocket so it would not be lost or misplaced. Nearing fifty, I was finding that my memory wasn't as good as it used to be. I could have put the key in a safe place but the way my memory had become I was sure that I would probably end up forgetting this safe place. It was as my uncle had said on his death-bed, as you get older everything seems to break-down: your eye-sight, hearing, memory and more. At times my memory had become so bad that I would walk into a room and forget why I'd gone there. Suffice to say in my case the key was safest in my pocket.

Having it uncomfortably in my pocket also served as a reminder that I needed to take a break from the farm and unravel the mystery of the safety-deposit box. Naturally, in the end, curiosity got the better of me and before I knew it I was on a plane heading for Auckland. Unfortunately in my haste, I had neglected to arrange to meet the diver who as it turned out was away on an overseas holiday. It was disappointing to miss him as I felt that he held the answers to the conundrum.

Having a window seat on the plane was a bonus as I had travelled very few times in my life by air. I spent most of the time glued to the window mesmerised by the stunning scenery below as the plane headed north. It followed the back-bone of the South Island — the snow-covered Southern Alps with their peaks, valleys and braided rivers.

"Wow, this view is amazing," I said turning to the passenger next to me, a similarly aged man who was working on a laptop.

"Gets to be quite boring when you travel this route for work every two or three weeks," he mumbled, hardly lifting his head.

"Well, this is a first for me as I spend most of my time on the farm and have no need or desire to travel," I replied.

The passenger grunted and returned to working on his laptop which he was balancing precariously against his bulging beer pot and the seat in front. I returned to surveying the scenery. The plane had now reached Cook Strait, the sea separating the two main islands. On my left I could see Farewell Spit stretching far out into the distance, curling like a big fish hook. After crossing the 23km of strait we continued flying north but now over the green, rolling hills, plains and valleys of the North Island.

"Wow, Mt Egmont. What a sight," I said, turning to the same passenger.

"Taranaki," he corrected. "It has been that now for some time ever since some obscure board, with nothing better to do with their time, decided to change the name."

"Yes, quite confusing when the plain is also called Taranaki," I replied. "I understand that this volcano was used in the filming of the Last Samurai because it looks so much like Mt Fuji."

The passenger didn't reply as he had already returned to his laptop and seemed to have more pressing things on his mind.

Not long after we started our gradual descent, breaking through some cloud to witness the awesome sight of the Manukau Harbour. We landed soon after at Auckland airport.

This was the first time that I'd flown to Auckland, so I trustingly followed the procession of departing passengers from the plane through a rabbit warren of passageways within the airport to a gathering of departing and arriving passengers. I pressed my way past chocked check-in areas to eventually find an airport exit sign directing me away from claustrophobic surroundings to awaiting buses and taxis. Outside the airport it was equally chaotic; a hive of activity as various buses and super shuttles arrived and departed, and taxi drivers waited for their next payload. Colin had already warned me that a taxi might cost more than the plane fare, so I started to look around for a bus that would transport me into the central city.

"Excuse me, can you tell me where I can get a bus into town?" I asked a well-built Maori man, who reminded me of a Sumo wrestler.

"Sky bus is over there, Bro," he pointed.

"Thanks, just such a busy place but I guess one can expect that for being both a domestic and international airport," I replied.

"This is domestic. You want international then it's ten minutes' walk that way, Bro." He pointed over towards a car parking building.

It was just as well that I took the bus as it seemed that I may have hit a peak period or was traffic always this congested in Auckland? It was a question that I was saving for Colin when I returned to Gore. The bus seemed to move more quickly down the busy roads often assisted by bus lanes. Once again I nervously fidgeted in my pocket to ensure that my uncle's safe key was still there next to my wallet, which of course it was. After arriving at the terminal all the fun started when I left the bus as I had no idea where I was or where I needed to go and Auckland central was such a noisy and busy place where I soon found that one jaywalked at their peril. Life here seemed to be at a faster impersonal pace as people moved briskly down footpaths and across roads; most, unlike Gore where one was bound to bump into someone you knew and stop for a chat. Around me buildings towered and invaded my space; an uncomfortable sense of claustrophobia to add to a sense of disorientation as I reluctantly pulled out my GPS and navigated my way to the bank.

Finally, I arrived and edged my way towards the bank's entrance, now developing a hot sweat, more from nervousness thinking of the task in hand, than the effort exerted in arriving at this destination. It was certainly not a warm day to produce such a sweat. What would the bank manager say when he or she found out that it wasn't my safe? Maybe they might turn me away or even call the police. I checked out the brochures at the information desk before finally plucking up enough courage to speak to the young woman behind the counter. She was pleasant, putting my mind somewhat at ease and she led me over to a smartly dressed man in a pin-stripe suit and tie sitting behind a desk and computer screen. I explained to him, as I produced the key, that this was my uncle's safe and that he was deceased. The man glared at me for a few seconds, with a piercing stare that seemed to search my very soul before he turned away and keyed something onto his computer.

"Ah, Robert, I take it?"

"Yes," I replied, somewhat relieved.

"ID?"

I fumbled in my pocket, pulling out a well-worn wallet, almost dropping the safe key in the process. I produced a driver's licence that had seen better days. He looked hard at me again this time comparing me to the faded photo.

"Any other ID?"

I gave him my credit card as well. He took both to the photocopying machine before returning.

"Follow me," he instructed as he led me through 'Fort Knox', a secure area with an iron-grill door. Inside were rows of small safe doors each with two keyholes. "Ah, this is the one," he said, poking his key into one of the keyholes then turning it. He beckoned for me to do likewise in the adjacent keyhole, then he pulled the heavy plated door open and drew out a long metal safety deposit box.

"Take this to the viewing room over there and press the button when you're ready to return it," he said, passing me the box.

I had anticipated that it might contain some gold bars but surprisingly it was nowhere near as heavy as expected. It was quite light and a disappointment, especially after all the effort in navigating my way to the bank. But now, finally, I would be able to discover the contents and just maybe find an answer to the General Grant. I waited until the man had left the room before anxiously selecting the smaller of the keys to open the padlock.

"I just hope this other key fits or it will be a wasted trip and an embarrassment," I said to myself, as I fumbled and finally managed to press the key into the padlock securing the safety deposit box. To my delight, the padlock miraculously sprung open. Now with trepidation, I took a deep breath before ever so slowly lifting the lid, my eyes peeled for what wonderful surprise might lie within. How many gold bars and what other treasure might I find?

My stomach dropped and my heart suddenly started deeply pounding as I sat motionless in shock. For a moment I thought I was going to have a heart attack as my eyes focused on a revolver, an illegal weapon without a special and restricted permit. With my eyes fixated on this object and anxiety setting in, I now broke out into a hot sweat and my body began to convulse. Could I be having a panic attack? I felt like cursing my uncle for raising my hopes and putting me through such an ordeal just for this. Why? And what was I to do with this gun as I could hardly walk out through the bank with it in my bag? I could hardly walk anywhere with it and I'd never pass through the metal detector at the airport. How was I to get rid of this thing; do I have to accept these contents as part of my inheritance or can I just walk away in denial?

My mind wandered to just who really was my uncle? Being raised on a farm, he was no stranger to guns, that is rifles, but this was a revolver. Most people on farms are familiar with rifles and shotguns. They're a necessity for killing pests like rabbits and possums and putting sick animals out of their misery. My uncle was a crack shot, probably as a result of his early years in the army, but I'm talking about shooting rifles, not a revolver. Why on earth would he have a revolver unless he was a criminal? I recalled when I was a youth that my uncle would often enjoy going off for a few days hunting in the mountains for deer, tahr, and pigs and he often returned successful, but that was with a rifle. My hands shook as I carefully brushed this object aside, careful not to add my fingerprints just in case this weapon had been used for criminal activities. It could even be a murder weapon.

"What the...?"

Beneath the gun were six passports: New Zealand, Canadian, British, American, Russian and German. Each had a picture of my uncle but with a different name. Now terrible thoughts rushed into my head. Perhaps my uncle was somebody sinister like an international hit-man. The fact was that he had never stayed with us for any length of time so did I really know him? I had always thought of him as a kind caring person and not as a cold-blooded, ruthless psychopath, but these were not the personal belongings of a treasure-hunter. It was a strange assortment of items to keep locked away in a bank vault knowing that one day I would be the one to find them. The treasure of the General Grant now looked most unlikely and just a tale, one to be replaced by some sinister narrative. Maybe all his treasure-hunting stories were untrue, even the pirate's treasure, despite what others had shared at his funeral. Yet at the bottom of the box were ten very old gold coins, a string of large pearls, and an ancient gold signet ring bearing a lion, all of which may have been recovered treasure. Buried under this was a gold Rolex watch and it seemed to be in good working order. This all just didn't make sense. I pushed the ring onto my finger and it fitted perfectly. The Rolex watch was heavy but was most welcome on my arm where I was determined it would stay. I deserved the ring and watch after having faced this terrible ordeal and I was sure that Mary would be delighted with the pearls. The final item was a red notebook with diagrams and writing that looked like code and made little sense. Maybe these were treasure sites that he had identified. I would take this home and see if my son, who was studying at university and was smarter than me, could crack the codes. I placed everything apart from the gun, passports, ring and watch into my backpack. Procrastination would be my solution to dealing with the gun and passports. As far as I was concerned they could remain in the bank safe and maybe someday never I'd decide what to do with them. For now, I preferred to be in denial that they ever existed. How could my uncle leave me with such a legacy and who was he?

Chapter 10

"Of all the liars in the world, the worst are our own fears."

Rudyard Kipling

At Dunedin airport Harry and Mary were there to meet me on my return from Auckland and to drive me back to Gore. I had already rehearsed a response in anticipation but instead of their inquiring about the contents of the safe and noticing the shiny additions to my wrist and finger, Harry had something more pressing on his mind.

"Dad, the floorboards have been lifted in Uncle's house and Jack seems to have vanished. Colin came and had a look but thought it pointless taking fingerprints because so many people had lived in that house."

"In my uncle's house you say and the floorboards?" I looked perplexed, but Jack vanishing was of no surprise. These transient workers tended to be like the wind coming and going, but why on earth would anyone lift the floorboards unless they thought that there could be something hidden underneath?

"Colin seems to think that Jack may have been looking for the gold, and Dad, the Friesian steer we'd been fattening up to kill has also disappeared."

"Probably keeled over in the paddock," I replied. "Have you searched in all the depressions and forested areas?"

"Dad, you'd smell a dead steer a mile away, and Mum and I have searched the whole farm anyway. It's been stolen and Colin thinks it was probably Jack. He's checking the local butchers."

"A Charolaise, maybe but a common Friesian, I'd hardly think so. How does he expect to tell one Friesian from another?"

"I did warn you about taking on a stranger and I knew the first time I laid eyes upon him that he was trouble with his shifty eyes," Mary voiced. "That's why I decided to come along with Harry. No way was I going to be left alone just in case that horrible man returns. He sends a shiver down my spine every time I see him and he did smell."

"That's a shame he's gone as we were getting a lot of the fencing sorted. He was a good, skilled worker." I waved my arm to see if anyone would notice my new watch. "Colin never liked the man either and is just making some wild accusations saying Jack tore up the floorboards and stole a steer."

"And perhaps he's right," replied Mary.

"Hey, whatever happened to the presumption of innocence until proven guilty? I'm not at all surprised that he's gone, Harry. I half expected him to one day just disappear without a word. And yes, Mary, Jack did ask me about the General Grant and he knew that Uncle lived in that cottage but I assured him that there was nothing in the rumours about my uncle finding the gold, which I'm now myself starting to believe as being the truth after my trip to Auckland."

"Good," replied Mary. "Now we can get on with life without all your ridiculous worry. I told you that there was no gold but you seemed to have had this belief ever since you were a young boy about your uncle and the General Grant treasure. It hasn't been pleasant living with you since your uncle died and you rekindled this obsession."

"He'd have no reason to pull up the floorboards," I continued, "and as for the steer, Jack would have at least needed an accomplice to move that brute. I think that Colin is wasting his time checking out the local butchers. The butchers know the local farmers and would have raised the alarm if a stranger came in wanting a beast cut up."

"That's what I thought too." Harry turned onto the highway. "Out with it, what's your news? We've all been dying to know what was in the safety deposit box, even Colin."

"More questions than answers," I replied, turning to Mary and once again flashing my watch, but still nobody seemed to notice. "I thought I knew my uncle but I was wrong. There's a couple of very old gold coins for you, Harry, and your brother; a ring and a watch for me and some pearls for you, Mary. It doesn't sound that much after all our expectations, but yes, I'm starting to believe that my uncle was not the treasure-hunter we believed him to be."

"Well, now we'll hopefully see an end to your anxiety," Mary smirked. "As I said, it hasn't been much fun living with Mr Anxiety. I'll take the pearls as compensation for what you've put me through."

"I wouldn't be too sure about it being an end to the anxiety," I replied as I remembered the gun, "and now I've got to face Colin with his 'I told you so'."

As expected, that evening Colin was anxiously waiting in the pub ready to draw blood. As I drew nearer he glared at me with disdain. I tried to keep off the subject by talking about how busy the roads were in Auckland but Colin wasn't going to be distracted.

"I warned you about sharing information about the gold," he said, banging his glass of beer down on the table and spilling some of the contents in the process. "This makes it a lot more difficult now for all of us when you find the gold."

"If it ever existed," I said.

"You're definitely going to need my involvement once you find it with the criminal world now alerted."

"But I never told Jack. In fact, I refuted what he'd heard from the pub." I picked up my glass and drank some beer. "Really, why would Jack remove the floorboards once I confirmed that the gold was a wild rumour? Yes, he was living in that cottage at the time but this could have also happened after he left."

"Well, you said that you'd told your pastor about the gold so I decided to do a bit more digging on him. It just so happens that in prison he was cellmates with Jack." Colin emptied his glass, very satisfied now that he had got his point across. "And I saw the two together the other day in town chatting."

"Oh! That's interesting." I gulped and turned a shade of pink. "Our pastor's a pretty chatty fellow who'll go out of his way to reach the community, especially those down and out like Jack. Maybe he was trying to persuade him to come to church. As for that steer, he was a large beast — well fattened for the kill, and Jack wouldn't have been able to move him on his own. If you've seen the weight the pastor carries then you'd understand that he'd be more of a hindrance than a help in moving that beast, let alone his own carcass. Then the transporting of the steer would've been a further problem. He may have a criminal record but I don't think Jack's your man."

"Anyhow, enough of you blabbing to anyone and everyone, I'm eager to know what was being held at the bank for your uncle. Gold bars I presume? Colin sat back in his chair, swirling the beer in his glass, waiting anxiously for the answer.

"No, a bit of an anti-climax I'm afraid. All this talk about my uncle and his treasure-hunting but there hasn't been much to show for it. Apart from this watch and ring, and some gold coins and a pearl necklace, the contents were disappointing."

"And a treasure map?" Colin asked as he eyed up my watch and ring with interest.

"Maybe, there was a red notebook but not easily decipherable if it is some map to a treasure." I emptied my glass. "Seriously, I'm now dubious about whether my uncle was ever a treasure-hunter. As for the General Grant's treasure, well that all looks to be just idle gossip."

"Well, there's a bit of money in that ring and the Rolex if it's not a cheap imitation," replied an envious Colin. "But you haven't changed, Robbie. Knowing you over many years, you've probably already laid hands on the gold. You always were rather crafty. So where have you got it hidden then? Maybe buried it in a paddock, or have you hidden it away in your barn?"

"Seriously, it's still probably somewhere on the sea-bed near the Auckland Islands I would suspect." I poured another glass. "Certainly it is less hassle there out of sight and out of mind."

"No, that doesn't wash with me," Colin muttered. "I've known you too long to know that's not true. When you're onto something you get all excited and want to tell the world, but when you find its true and realise the implications then you go very quiet. Based on the war stories at your uncle's funeral he was very much a treasure-hunter and I for one, given your uncle's experience and tenacity, find it hard to believe that he didn't find the General Grant's treasure. If anyone was going to find it then it would be him. You need to be upfront with me, Robbie, especially now the criminal world is involved. There could be very rough times ahead and you need, more than anything, the police on your side."

"Perhaps the accountant might shed some light if there is any gold," I commented. "I'm off to meet with him and the IRD on Monday."

"IRD? Well, the best of luck. You may need it," laughed Colin. Just remember Al Capone."

Chapter 11

"They can't collect legal taxes from illegal money."

Al Capone

Driving to Christchurch was a long and boring experience, the flat Canterbury plains and long straight roads offering little to the eye. The snow-clad Southern Alps on my left though made for a pleasant view and occasionally the monotony of the journey was broken by a small town.

"Good to finally meet you, Robert," said the accountant, a slightly greying man in his mid-forties. The accountant stood up, reached across the desk, and extended his hand. "Now, your uncle said you were a Southland farmer. I guess like everyone else these days you're into dairying? Seems to be where the money is, though the environmentalists are very much against it."

"Gore is Romney country," I replied. "Though we do run a small herd of Angus-Hereford cross, but not for milking."

"Herd of cows?" The accountant laughed.

"No, but I've heard of sheep," I replied, smirking. "Romney is a long wool sheep and originated in Kent, England. Gore is the New Zealand home of Romney."

"Ah, ha, one of the farmers of our 40 million sheep." The accountant returned to his seat, quite pleased he had shown he had some knowledge on the subject.

"I believe that it may now be 60 million sheep in New Zealand and just under 5 million people. On those statistics, you'd think that we'd all be sheep farmers." I laughed as I pulled up a chair and sat down. "I guess I should have worn a suit for this meeting," I said, noting my casual appearance against the accountant's stunning grey pinstriped tailor-made suit and matching shirt and tie. He was immaculately dressed.

"Ha, not these days, my friend," chuckled the accountant. "I'm afraid professionalism has sadly all but gone out the window. The tax investigator is bound to be yet another government woolly jumper. These days their dress sense, like some of my colleagues, has become rather shabby and unbecoming. This is despite many of these people being chartered accountants, members of my profession." The accountant tapped the desk with his pen, obviously a rather irritating habit he had fallen into. "Is this your first interview with the IRD, Robert?"

"Yes, a bit of a worry. I'm not sure what to expect especially since this is all about my uncle's stuff."

"Exactly." The accountant stopped and paused for a moment.

"What do you know about your uncle's activities, like his income and investments?"

"Absolutely nothing," I replied. "My uncle was very secretive. I don't know why I need to be here and how I can be of any help."

"Excellent, so that's all you need to tell the IRD. I have dealt with them on many occasions, so leave it to me to answer the questions and don't volunteer any information or thoughts, OK? Once the IRD has finished, and we've sent the investigator packing, we will have a good chat regarding your uncle's investments."

"So what's this investigation about anyway?" I enquired. "I don't understand how they're involved when my uncle is dead."

The accountant looked at me, also puzzled. "Well, I guess there's still his estate. The IRD never disclose their reasons for investigating but I suspect…"

There was a knock at the door and a tall elderly man walked in.

"Greg, good to see you again, take a seat. This is Sir Gregory Brown," announced the accountant. "He was your uncle's business partner and agreed to also attend the interview."

"Yes, we've met," I replied, shaking his hand.

"Good to meet you again," said Gregory giving me a wink.

"I've already instructed Robert to say nothing, Greg," the accountant added.

"Definitely, best leaving it to us as these investigators will latch onto anything you say. They're very smart," agreed Gregory. "Best just giving a straight yes or no, Robbie. Well, that's always been my strategy and it has always worked."

"Good, we're all in agreement then?" The accountant picked up the phone to ask his receptionist to bring in the investigator.

The investigator was a young man in his thirties, in a woolly jumper but tidily dressed. After the initial introductions and shaking of hands, he immediately let everyone know that he was in charge and he would be recording our answers to his questionnaire.

"Now, I'm somewhat perplexed, as in researching your client's history I note that over his lifetime he has never returned any income." The investigator looked firmly at the accountant.

"That's correct as he was over that time a non-resident." The accountant smiled.

"Yet he has a New Zealand accountant?"

"And what's wrong with that?" replied the accountant. "He may want to invest in New Zealand shares or property. He may likewise have had accountants overseas investing other money in other countries at times."

"Which leads me to the question of where did your uncle live?" the investigator asked, turning towards me.

"Well, before he died he was in a Rest Home," I replied. "But not by choice," I added.

Gregory smirked because he would have guessed that my uncle would have hated every minute of being in a Rest Home.

"No, I mean before that," said the investigator.

"He lived on cruise ships overseas. My uncle was an adventure seeker," I added. "When he felt he was beyond going on overseas adventures he resorted to cruise ships. It was only after he reached a poor state of health that he reluctantly agreed to a Rest Home and at that stage, he was on his death-bed."

"And before that?"

"I seldom saw my uncle as he was most of the time overseas, but when he was in New Zealand he stayed on the farm."

"Yes, he was in New Zealand less than 183 days in any twelve-month period," added the accountant.

"So then what did he use for transport when he stayed with you?" asked the investigator.

"He just borrowed one of our farm vehicles as he didn't own any of his own. It's a family farm and he came and went as he pleased."

"So he owned part of the farm then?"

"No, my dad bought out his share Gran left him many, many years ago, thanks to a legacy left from my Great Aunt Betty. My uncle was never interested in farming."

"Great Aunt Betty?" The investigator looked puzzled.

"Look we're talking fifty years ago or more when as I understand a relative overseas left Rob's parents money in her will," explained the accountant who had turned slightly pink.

"Oh, I see." The investigator looked down at his questionnaire. "So what type of work did your uncle do overseas?"

"I wouldn't have a clue. He was very secretive but he loved travelling and adventure; that's all I know."

The investigator turned to my uncle's accountant. "So what type of work did he do overseas?"

"How would I know?" replied the accountant. "I just advised him on investments."

"So what do you know about the General Grant, then?" the investigator asked the accountant.

"The General Grant? Are you talking about that old sailing boat that came to grief on the Auckland Islands?" the accountant asked.

"Yes," replied the investigator.

"Not a great deal, I'm an accountant, not a historian. That was some time in the eighteen hundreds, well before I was born. What on earth has that got to do with my client?" the accountant snapped.

"General Grant?" I repeated, meeting a death-threatening glare from the accountant.

"You know something then?" asked the investigator, turning to me.

"Only I heard that somebody had carried out a salvage attempt a few years ago and found nothing." I looked back at the accountant who seemed now less likely to kill me. "Wasn't there supposed to be gold on it when it sunk?"

"Did you find the treasure, Mr Brown?" asked the investigator.

"Sir Gregory," barked the accountant, who leapt at an opportunity to put the investigator on defence. "Have some respect. This man has a knighthood."

"Sorry, Sir Gregory, but did you recover the gold since you were, as I understand it, a partner?"

"From the Auckland Islands? Are you suggesting that I would foolishly risk taking my yacht into those dangerous waters when there are easier and safer options like gold-bearing wrecks lying off the calmer, warmer waters of eastern Australia?" Gregory contorted his face. "Have you any idea how many boats have come to grief off the Auckland Islands and goodness knows how many people have perished in those icy Sub-Antarctic waters, including a number searching for the treasure? Where on earth did you get such a ridiculous idea from, man?"

"Probably an anonymous source, I would think," suggested the accountant, looking towards the investigator who now displayed a pinkish complexion. "So this is the reason for wasting our time? Sir Gregory is a busy man, a director on many company boards and he has flown all the way from Auckland for this interview, and poor Robert here has had to leave the responsibility of his farm and family and drive up from Gore."

"Was it some anonymous source?" asked Gregory.

The investigator with a poker face didn't reply or make eye contact.

"So you've wasted our time on some hunch from some troublemaker?" continued Gregory. "You need to realise that in my business I make many enemies and I would've expected the IRD to first decipher between fact and fiction instead of wasting our time."

"No good asking him," said the accountant. "They're not allowed to reveal their sources of information which, in this case, is undoubtedly from malicious people trying to retaliate for one reason or another as you suggested. When people are as secretive as Robert's uncle was they'll go to any lengths to find answers and learn his secrets."

"All you needed to do was to check the mooring records held at Bluff and Oban and you will find that I have never ever used those ports," continued Gregory. "One would have to be foolish to venture into the Southern Ocean without first letting the authorities know. If we didn't and came to grief then we'd be goners."

Gregory, now with a red complexion, cleared his throat before continuing. "Have you any idea what such a salvage operation in those turbulent frigid waters would require and you think that two or three of us could just sail away south into unpredictable seas and try our luck; a treasure which could now, with the strong currents and rough seas, be scattered anywhere after a hundred years."

"It's unbelievable that you could have even believed this." The accountant frowned at the investigator.

"As far as I know," said Gregory, "the last salvage operation was in the mid-nineties and was not just a simple operation as you would suggest. There was something like a dozen divers and because the water is so cold in the Southern Ocean they had hot water pumping around their suits. The divers found that the wreck had disintegrated and in order to search the sandy seabed they first needed to remove rocks and winch huge boulders off the bottom. This was a very expensive and laborious operation, far beyond two or three people, which I presume you are suggesting. They found nothing, which is what I'd expect given that the General Grant's location was known and surely at least one of the many salvage attempts over the last hundred years would have been successful."

The investigator, now in recovery mode, quickly changed the subject and moved to questions about the farm before ending by saying, "I've recorded your answers to these questions on this interview sheet. Please can you check these and if satisfied sign them as true and correct."

I looked towards the accountant, who nodded. We all, in turn, signed the questionnaire before returning it to the investigator.

"I'll have a copy of that," said the accountant aggressively.

"So will I," demanded Gregory. "This is outrageous."

The accountant called in his receptionist who took away the interview notes for copying.

Chapter 12

"Figures don't lie but liars figure."

Mark Twain

After Gregory and the investigator had left the room, the accountant leaned back into his chair. A large smile crossed his face.

"Well, that's done and dusted." The accountant rubbed his hands. "You've got to play hardball with these investigators and put them on the back foot or otherwise they'll be all over you, poking their nose into areas they don't belong. I rather enjoyed that and we came out on top."

"You seemed to be rather hard on the investigator calling Gregory Sir Gregory," I said, smirking.

"Part of the game of getting the upper hand. He'll now go away fearing that Greg may lay a complaint with the Department and he will. Greg has his reputation at stake and that is why he took a copy of the investigator's notes. He wouldn't want people thinking that he found the treasure and dodged paying taxes on this. Give it a week or two with Greg involved and we should get a letter saying the audit has been completed and you'll be able to have your money." The accountant laughed. "This knighthood rubbish does now and again come in quite handy, though I don't have much time for it myself."

"You don't?" I looked surprised, given all the kerfuffle.

"Of course not. I guess there are some worthy of the recognition, but the whole thing is a farce and the title quite meaningless when you add dodgy businessmen and politicians to this group. But for people like Greg, it opens the doors to an elite group and is a great cover for all his dodgy dealings. Greg and I have often had a laugh about it over a beer."

"So, they found the General Grant, then did they?" I had to put the question. It seemed to me that both the accountant and Greg might be hiding something.

"Robert, I know nothing," replied the accountant, "absolutely nothing." He went a shade of pink. "Though I wouldn't put it past Greg. He's a crafty one and has the right connections to get his knighthood. It was always a mystery how he, coming from a poor family, came by all his wealth."

"Shady?" I looked inquisitively at the accountant.

"Definitely, I'd say so," replied the accountant, "but so too is your uncle's lawyer. I didn't tell you this, but in the interview, you referred to Great Aunt Betty. Well, she never existed."

"Sorry, what do you mean never existed? Of course, she existed." I looked at the accountant, surprised. "My dad got all that money from her."

"Fabricated, Robert, I'm afraid to say. At a young age, your uncle became extremely rich when he found buried treasure. After that, he didn't need the half share in the farm. Great Aunt Betty was a way he could give your father the other half of the farm without paying the tax department gift duty. As I understand it, his solicitor had a colleague in England who did all the paperwork creating the legacy, then he sent the cheque. The money followed a circular path from your uncle to London then from London to Dunedin with of course hefty solicitor fees being paid. The solicitors, putting their necks on the line, did it at a premium and made a killing as they always do."

"Sounds fraudulent to me." I looked shocked.

"Absolutely," replied the accountant. "Corruption is epidemic and only a fool would believe otherwise. It's a question of what you can get away with. But I don't know anything about this, OK?"

"Did my father know or did he go to his grave ever thankful for Great Aunt Betty?"

"I'm sure that he wouldn't have known. Your uncle said he was a proud man and would never have accepted the money otherwise."

"So what work did my uncle do overseas?" I asked.

"Seriously, that I don't know. Your uncle was very tight-lipped about everything. All I know about is the money he invested, as I told the investigator." The accountant reached across his desk to drag a file towards him.

"Did the solicitor tell you how much money you inherited and that it is currently invested in the Cayman Islands?" asked the accountant.

"He told me the amount but not where it is invested. Isn't that a tax haven?" I must have looked concerned and once again I felt another reason to feel anxious. My uncle was starting to look more and more like a shady character. On top of this, his partner, accountant and lawyer also all looked dodgy. Then there were the passports. Perhaps my uncle was somehow tied up in the criminal world and if so, was I now in danger and were these other characters also members?

"Of course it's a tax haven," laughed the accountant. "Look, my job as an accountant is to minimise tax and get the best return for my client. If you don't need the money then I can just roll these investments over but now in your name. It will be no trouble and you'll have tax-free income. It would certainly make my job easier."

"No, I'll take all the money. I have plans on replacing my tractor, the car and other things and I don't want any investments in the Cayman Islands. Mary, my wife, would have a fit if she knew my uncle had his money invested there." I started to shake at the thought of having to look over my shoulder waiting for the next IRD audit, or worse, a policeman knocking at the door. I could do without this stress in my life.

"OK, it seems that you've made up your mind." The accountant didn't look overly happy. "I guess you'll now be off back to Gore without taking in the sights of our post-earthquake city."

"No, I wasn't sure how long I'd be tied up for so I thought I'd play it safe and have the whole afternoon to explore. What I've seen so far are a lot of empty sections."

"Yes, and that's after eight years. The rebuild is very slow. Our cathedral is still in ruins and the new buildings seem to be mostly glass. On top of that, the council is intent on messing up the roads by making them narrow with bicycle lanes that you could drive a bus through. It would have been the perfect opportunity to run a train through the centre of town joining the railway on both sides of the city, but no, they seem to be missing some of the most pragmatic improvements."

"I don't like the idea of a railway down the centre of the road." I screwed up my face at the thought. "That could be rather hazardous for cars and pedestrians."

"No, it would be above the road as they have done in Bangkok. It would be so easy to do, especially when they have plenty of road width to waste on bicycle lanes."

"But Christchurch doesn't have the population to support rail," I said.

"Well, it's bigger than Newcastle in England and their system is well supported. In the future, the population in Christchurch will be even larger and they'll face the same problems Auckland is now facing in establishing an inner-city rail. If Auckland had only listened to Mayor Robbie in the 1980s they would have saved millions."

"Yes, I believe a man well ahead of his time," I replied. "I remember him well."

"So, you were in Christchurch when the earthquake hit?" I asked.

"Yes, on the fourth story. It wasn't much fun as my chair rocked back and forth and my computer keyboard was flung onto the floor. After the earthquake, many accountants relocated to the suburbs, our clients unhappy about going back into the inner city and scared of any multi-story building and lifts."

"Really?"

"In fact, with all the continued aftershocks, I was tempted to return to Auckland except my client base, built up over many years, was in Christchurch." The accountant tapped the desk again with his pen.

"So you're an Aucklander?" I asked.

"Yes, in fact, Greg was one of my first clients up in Auckland, but he's no longer a client." The accountant looked up at the clock on the wall. "Oh my next client's appointment was due five minutes ago and he must be getting rather annoyed out there in the waiting room." The accountant stood up and shook my hand before I left his office.

Chapter 13

"We were all humans until race disconnected us, religion separated us, politics divided us and wealth classified us."

Anonymous

When I first mentioned the possibility of taking a trip to Bali, Mary was very supportive.

"We must go, after all, you can't deny your uncle his death-bed wish, especially after making you his sole beneficiary," she replied. "And I'm more than happy to join you and support you and you needn't worry at all about me. I'm sure that the local shops and hotel facilities will keep me fully occupied while you go about your business."

She was excited about going to Bali, even though I did not share the same sentiment. I was a rural lad and content just day to day bumping along on my farm where I was my own boss deciding on what I would do each day and when I'd take breaks. There was never any pressing need to visit and breathe in the polluted air of some over-populated country when I had the pure pollution-free air of the Southland countryside. It reminded me of what I had heard about large cities like Auckland: the busy streets, noise and smell, but Bali, I imagined, would be substantially worse. Indonesia, I had heard, was one of the most densely populated areas in the world and I could envisage Mary and me pushing our way through crowded pavements and being driven down congested petrol polluted roads. I had absolutely no desire for this experience. Everything I needed was at home like enjoying the occasional family barbeque under a starry night sky, a sky so pristine-clear that you could even observe falling stars and watch satellites tracking across our corner of the world. Why on earth would I want to sacrifice any of this, even just for a short period, to visit some Third World country? My life-views were certainly quite contradistinctive to that of my adventuresome uncle. An overseas trip seemed absurd when just within a day's travel from my home I had everything: lakes, rivers, mountains and the sea.

Mary was also a rural lass and at home on a farm. But I guess being stuck in a farmhouse a large part of 24/7 was no fun, though she did get to visit town when she felt like it and on occasions she travelled further afield to shop at New Zealand's southern-most city, Invercargill. She had a great life with little to complain about. From Mary's comments, it seemed that this time she was going to make the most of her get-out-of-prison-free card and planned on a big spending-spree in Bali. She had heard that prices were very cheap from a number of her friends that had been there. From these conversations, she had prepared a list of things she intended to buy. Regretfully, I had yet to pluck up the courage to mention that due to a mistake, I had made in booking the flights, we were limited only to carry-on luggage. To purchase check-in luggage now would be ridiculous, costing an arm and a leg, and it just wasn't worth it. Anyhow there should be ample room in her carry-on luggage for what clothes she needed over the seven days away.

Mary, not surprisingly, was not at all pleased by my news, and on one occasion I thought that I might be relegated to the lounge sofa. A total over-reaction on her part, I thought, to a minor variation in our travel plans.

"Well, you'll have to take old clothes and you can throw them away when you're over there. I'll be having your bag as well for all my purchases," she stormed.

I would have thought that she'd get over it but for the next week I was not at all in her good books and I spent more time pottering out on the farm and picking my moments to return inside for a cuppa. The woman should have been more grateful as this much cheaper flight only took twelve hours when many of the other flights took much longer and having only carry-on baggage had the advantage of ensuring that nothing was planted in our suitcases. Bali had been on the news many times recently with stories of people being apprehended for carrying drugs and facing the death penalty or long prison sentences. Some had claimed that the drugs had been planted. Mary, however, was not convinced by my rationalisation and in her opinion, these travellers were using the only excuse they could having been caught red-handed.

As it was, I found the flight quite long and boring. Being cooped up on a plane was no fun for a farming lad used to stretching out his legs on a few hundred acres of paddock, and on a few occasions racing the bull to the gate. It was preposterous that the airline staff expected you to eat food from a tray extending out from the seat in front and with plastic utensils more fitting for toddlers. It only needed the person in front to recline their seat for the food to end up on one's lap. Then you were stuck with all the empty containers until an air hostess arrived to clear them. Why it took so long was mind-boggling but I suspect they had to allow extra time for older passengers, especially those with false teeth, to finish their meals.

The arrival at the airport was just as bad: the queues; the paperwork and the prying eyes of customs officials as if we were all criminals. Fortunately, I had not hired a car from the airport as it appeared to be pure anarchy on the roads; the taxi on one occasion scraping past other cars in a free-for-all intersection. From the car window, the surroundings were definitely Third World. Dingy buildings lined the street and the vehicles using them seemed to be of an older vintage. Finally, we reached our hotel, the Ibis Styles, Denpasar, which surprisingly looked quite nice and no different to any other hotel in the handful I had stayed in previously. The room was quite pleasant with a balcony looking out towards the road.

"It has a swimming pool," announced my excited wife, who had been for a wander around the hotel. "But more importantly it also has free transport to and from Hardy's and Bali Collection. They're meant to be good shopping places with lots of variety and bargains."

"That's good, then I won't need to accompany you, as long as you're sure that this is safe. There is a dark side to Bali and you don't want to wander off into some dodgy area and end up minus a few organs."

"It's door to door and Hardy's is all one shop." She started to sort through her suitcase. "But I may need you to accompany me to Bali Collection as this involves many shops over a large area."

For me, apart from flying long distances, there was nothing worse than the embarrassment of shopping in the women's clothing department. The thought of accompanying her at Bali Collection was therefore not appealing.

"Tomorrow I think I'll go shopping at Hardy's." Mary looked pleased. "And you, Robbie?"

"Oh, I'm here to catch up with my uncle's ex-business partner, though as you know I'm not thrilled about the prospect. His name is Wally Devine and he lives in our hotel. I'm not sure how he's going to respond given that my uncle ran away with his girlfriend."

"Welcome to Bali, Mr Anxiety," laughed Mary. "Come on, you're scared of a man who must now be in his eighties. I'm sure that you'll be safe. No doubt after that episode he's probably had more exciting chapters in his life. From what you told me he was well rid of Martha and your uncle probably did him a favour."

"Yes, you're probably right," I murmured, as I emptied my suitcase. "I think we should take a walk before dark and find a currency exchange and a place to eat tonight," I suggested.

"Well, there's plenty of currency exchange places I noticed as we came down the street to our hotel. My friends warned me not to go to just any. They suggested something established like a shop." Mary placed some of her clothes on the bed.

"Good, then let's get started. I need to stretch my legs after such a long flight."

Outside it was very hot and humid and it quickly became apparent that I was no longer braving a Southland winter. As we walked down the street on a tar-sealed footpath we noticed many eating places and money changers. After changing our money we decided on an eating place and were thrilled to find that a good meal cost a third of the price we'd have paid in New Zealand. If prices were that cheap for food then what would be the case for souvenirs, clothing and other items? I suddenly became concerned about our suitcase situation and the fact that Mary was off shopping the next day. Maybe if the worst came to worst we could post parcels back but postage was now expensive as well.

The next day Mary was on a high, and I have to say I was as well, at the prospect of a buffet breakfast.

"I love buffet breakfasts," I announced.

"At your age, you should be cutting down." Mary looked concerned and patted my bulging lower abdomen.

"I'm a growing lad," was my reply.

Mary glared at me. "Yes, it's a shame. You need to take better care of yourself or you'll start to look like our pastor."

"I do love bacon and eggs," I said, as we entered the breakfast room.

"You need to order the bacon," Mary said, as she read a notice board. "And the man over there in the corner cooks eggs to your requirements."

"Strange having to order the bacon," I replied.

"Not strange at all." Mary looked across at some women wearing head scarfs. "Bali is part of Indonesia which is a Muslim country. Ironically, there are more Hindu than Muslim in Bali and I guess they make accommodation for Muslim and others who don't eat pork."

I settled down to a hearty breakfast before having to move out of my comfort zone and meet Wally Devine. Perhaps he was one of the elderly men I had seen in the breakfast room. If he looked as spent as some of these guests then he would be a pushover.

In many ways, I was looking forward to our meeting as I was now very confused about the General Grant and who my uncle was. More importantly what happened to the gold if they salvaged it? Perhaps this man might share his secrets or would he too take them to his grave?

Chapter 14

"Life is a shipwreck but we must not forget

tossing in the lifeboats."

Voltaire

Wally Devine was sunbathing on one of the many beach loungers lining the beach. He was not easy to find as I had to first cross the road from the hotel and walk down through a long narrow alleyway next to the Travel Lodge Hotel to reach the seaside. I had worrying thoughts during the short journey down the alleyway. What if I reached halfway only to find that I was being followed and other thugs were coming from the other direction? One thing was for sure, it ruled out a romantic night time walk to the beach even if Mary insisted.

The tanned muscular torso of the eighty-plus-year-old, spread out over a bench lounger, looked far from spent and of a much younger biological age. He was a large, strongly built man and somewhat as intimidating as he would have been in his prime. There was nothing wrong with his hearing as he turned to see who was whooshing through the sand towards his personal space. Wally remained prostrate, untroubled by my approach, and lazily raised his sunglasses to improve his view of this approaching stranger.

"Wally Devine?" I asked.

"And what's it to you mate if I am?" he thundered back. "Who the hell might you be? Come closer man so I can see you more clearly."

"My uncle sent me. He used to be your partner on treasure-hunting expeditions," I said, as I moved up within a metre of his beach lounger.

"Ah, not another sheep shagger? So where's that two-faced scoundrel then?" Wally suddenly lurched forward and grabbed my arm in a vice-like grip, rendering my arm useless. "Steals my sheila and my booty and leaves me on my own to sail home and now he sends his nephew instead of being a man and coming in person. Why can't he be a man and come himself?"

"He's dead."

Wally's face dropped and he released my arm.

"Dead, you say?" He looked concerned. "When did this happen?"

"Yes, dead, a few months ago. It was his death-bed wish that I see you."

"So, what have you got for me, man?" Wally sat upright. "Where is it?"

"Got for you? No, he sent me to explain about Martha. Apparently, it had weighed heavily on him all these years and he wanted you to know that it was her idea to leave and she was the one who took your share of the treasure. She used my uncle as well just to get away, then she dumped him."

"You didn't bring it? Oh yes, that would be good old Martha, even after I saved her from a fate worth than death. To think what those men would have done to her." Wally now looked less belligerent and more at ease.

"That's the part I don't understand," I replied. "I know my uncle would never talk about his last trip with you. He seemed terrified and it seems that he and Martha just wanted to get away from whatever it was. So what happened?"

Wally laughed, "Haha, it wasn't all that bad, just a case of low-lives getting their just desserts. There were winners all around. The tiger sharks got a good feed and I did a service to the local community."

"So what happened, or are you going to be tight-lipped just like my uncle?"

Wally beckoned for me to take the next beach chair and he stretched back down to soak up the sun.

"Tell me how your uncle died," he asked, as he settled back into position on the lounger.

"Old age caught up with him, I'm sorry to say. Up until recently, he had been fighting fit taking cruises around the world then a few months ago he had a stroke. After that his health deteriorated very quickly and the pneumonia finished him off."

"Well, I'll be, the poor old bugger. If nothing else gets you pneumonia will. To think of his colourful life; the adventures and the number of bullets he dodged to finally reach an old age. We had some great times together and I'll miss him even if he could be a pain at times. Thank goodness that I'm still fit and able to enjoy my freedom."

"Yes, he hated it in a Rest Home."

"No, not a Rest Home? You didn't put him in a Rest Home? For a man like your uncle that would be very cruel." Wally lay still for a few minutes and glared at me. "Fair dinkum, a Rest Home? How could you do that to your own flesh and blood?"

"I know, but I had no choice. He needed 24-hour care," I replied.

"You know, he wasn't such a bad old bugger. Yes, he had his faults but I always thought Martha was to blame even if she was a skippy."

"Skippy?" I asked.

"Australian, man. Don't you know anything? Is she still alive?"

"Yes, apparently she was at his funeral but didn't want to be noticed."

Your uncle did us all a favour taking Martha away," continued Wally. "Just a shame how such good times came to an abrupt end but we had many great adventures. I see you have his Rolex," Wally added, as he eyed up the large gold watch on my wrist. "I was with him when he bought it. Best not to wear it around Bali unless you want to be mugged. You only have to have two hundred Aussie dollars here and you're a millionaire, and with that watch, you'd make the top of the list for a mugging. Plenty of places here that will clean it up for you very cheaply so it will once again look the part."

"So, what happened? Why did my uncle and Martha leave you?"

"I have to give it to you, mate, you're as persistent as your uncle and you're not going to stop hounding me, are you young man? I guess this is one story that I can now share." Wally pulled himself up onto his chair and rubbed some suntan lotion over his chest, smothering the line of grey hairs running down the centre. His chest was pitted with white blotches where he had lost skin pigment over the years. He pointed over towards his left to where the coastline stretched out to the sea.

"Do you know that's a volcano over there? Mt Gunung Agung, they call it. Had five eruptions in 2017. These islands of Indonesia are covered in volcanoes, some quite devastating like Krakatoa. Now Krakatoa is interesting when…."

"Your story?" I interjected, having taken off my tee-shirt and settling myself down on the next beach lounger.

"OK," he replied. "You're not unlike your uncle, a man with tenacity. I have never told this story before."

Chapter 15

"Greed makes man blind and foolish, and

makes an easy prey for death."

Rumi

"My story goes way back to the early 1960s. They were good years when your uncle and I were young and fit and Martha had legs on her that would turn any man's head." Wally began clearing his throat. "Martha had done some research and located an area where a Spanish galleon had come to grief after being caught in a hurricane."

"So where was that?" I asked.

"Near one of the Caribbean Islands," replied Wally.

"Look, there are over twenty islands in the Caribbean, so which one?" I asked.

"You don't need to know," Wally growled in his deep voice. "Do you want to hear the story or not?"

"Yes, please continue," I replied.

"Anyway, on our treasure hunts, Martha's expertise was in researching out possible areas of wrecks. She would go through archives in libraries and search records in other places and this might take weeks. Your uncle's job was researching out the local sea currents, and weather patterns and from this data calculating where the wreckage might have drifted to. You see a ship might sink in one spot but the sea current over time may spread the wreckage and cover it with debris. My job was both captain of our sailing boat and the main diver; you could say the only diver. Martha never dived and while your uncle could and did occasionally he wasn't comfortable being underwater. Initially, he would have to accompany me as we needed to cover a fairly wide area to first locate evidence of a wreck. Once it was found I was left to carry out the retrieval of the spoils while your uncle from the deck pulled up the spoils and monitored the equipment."

"And Martha?"

"Oh, Martha! That sheila was a bludger, but in her opinion had already done her part researching for wrecks. She was quite happy to sunbathe in her brief yellow bikini on the deck, while we did all the work. But she still expected her third of the booty."

"Anyhow, we spent several days in the area looking for this wreck before we found it but it was now drawing near the end of the day. Your uncle returned to the surface leaving me to brush away muck on the seafloor in search of what might be buried by the sands of time. Unfortunately, when you start stirring up the bottom it starts to pollute the water around you and obscure your vision. It was just lucky that I detected a large shape moving towards me."

"A shark?" I suggested.

"Not just any shark. Most sharks are not a worry but this was a five-metre man-eating tiger shark."

"So you quickly returned to the surface?" I asked.

"Hell no, do you think I'm crazy, man?" replied Wally. "That'd be suicidal. Sharks have poor vision, so it's best to keep very still and pray it will not detect you and will pass by. I couldn't ascend to the surface quickly anyway without the risk of the bends. If the shark didn't get me first then I could easily have died of decompression sickness."

"The shark, what happened?"

"Fortunately, the shark changed direction as they often do and homed in on an injured dolphin. My immediate thoughts were to ascend while the tiger shark was occupied and before the feeding frenzy began as this would draw in other sharks. What was very clear to me was that there could now be no more diving that day. As it turned out we were low on food supplies anyway and we needed to go to the island to stock up. After purchasing all our supplies we decided to have a pint or two at one of the local pubs as diving can get to be thirsty work. It turned out to be a bad move as a very dangerous man on the island, I'll call him Carlos, walked in with his bodyguard."

"So who's Carlos?" I asked.

"Was," laughed Wally. "He was a right drongo with political connections; his brother a very powerful person on the island who had seen many people murdered and tortured. We knew who he was and we quickly attempted to leave before we became outnumbered by his band of thugs. Your uncle, Martha and I had quickly downed our beers, but before we could leave he approached our table. He was quite aggressive and demanded to know what our business was. Your uncle told him that we were divers interested in the undersea world and shipwrecks. The bugger then placed his large hand on the back of your uncle's chair, pressing his knuckles hard into his shoulder. Your uncle wincing in pain then added that we had tried a bit of exploratory diving earlier that day but got scared off by a tiger shark. The big man thought that very funny and told us that those sharks out there got very hungry with the fishermen taking all their fish. He warned us that if we didn't want to end up as shark food then we better let him know if we find any treasure. Your uncle agreed to and the big man removed his hand."

"My uncle did nothing?" I looked shocked.

"Look mate, we were on their turf and they were the law. It was a case of making the best out of a bad situation. And there was no way we were going to tell him if we found treasure. Anyhow Carlos moved back to his table then, first swearing at the barmaid and reducing her to tears, demanded that she bring him a couple of beers. He placed his hand on her bum then laughingly shoved her in the direction of the bar. We quickly took the opportunity to leave and take the boat out to sea as fast as we could sail. Your uncle watched to see we weren't followed but, at a guess, binoculars would have been focused on us until we disappeared into the horizon. It would not be difficult, if they were interested, for them to locate our anchorage and we suspected that it would only be a few days before Carlos paid us a visit to claim our booty. We needed to move fast. He was the type of person who would wait and let us do all the work then come along with his thugs and take the booty and probably still feed us to the sharks."

"Early the next morning we commenced the operation of retrieving the treasure. That day we recovered gold and silver coins, some jewellery and a lot of old pottery and other historic but valueless items. It was late in the afternoon, when as I was loading treasure for your uncle to hoist up, that the same large tiger shark reappeared. From a distance, I could see it clearly, its broad flat head and long bluish-grey slender body with faded black vertical stripes. Fortunately, this time it was much further away, but it was an opportune time to resurface. At this point, I want to give you your uncle's account of what happened."

"Martha was on board sunbathing in her yellow bikini as usual and your uncle was on board waiting for my two tugs on the rope to say haul it up. Your uncle suddenly noticed, in the distance, a large yellow launch speeding towards them. Martha quickly got dressed and your uncle hid the gold, silver and valuable items in a secret compartment we had especially made should such a situation arise. We also had a revolver hidden in the wall. Your uncle left broken pieces of pottery and some less valuable items on the deck to convince the visitors that we had found the wreck but nothing of value. Now back to my story."

"Yes, the tiger shark," I reminded Wally. "And you surfaced?"

"Well, the shark wasn't a problem this time as I ascended, but as the hull of our boat came into view I noticed the hull of a second boat on the port side. I quickly dived back down to the collection of booty I had attached to the rope and replaced it with non-valuable heavy items like pieces of the shipwreck and a cannonball. Checking that the shark hadn't returned I gave the rope two tugs then ascended on the starboard side. I was able to slip onto the boat unnoticed as all attention was focused on the portside trying to pull up a very heavy booty. If there had been a guard on my side then he would have been reassigned to the portside as pulling up this load required many hands. Slipping into the cabin unnoticed I retrieved the revolver and from the cabin window, I was able to assess the situation. Carlos was quite excited, standing on the deck throwing the orders around, anxious to lay his hands on the treasure. Another man was holding a revolver pressed against your uncle's head and the other was helping your uncle, both with their arms fully stretched trying to pull up the rope. Carlos's right-hand man, who had been with him in the pub, had other intentions and was holding Martha uncomfortably with his arms around her chest. His manhandling of Martha made me very angry and I decided that he should take the first bullet. I slid out of the cabin unnoticed and planted a bullet between his eyes and within seconds, before the man with the gun against your uncle's head could pull the trigger, he too lay prostrate on the deck. The man helping your uncle turned around in surprise just in time to fall to the third bullet and your uncle had no alternative, given the weight, but to release the rope and send the booty crashing down to the bottom. Your uncle and Martha, now no longer prisoners, looked over towards the big man, Carlos."

"And probably no longer the big tough guy," I said.

"Exactly, a total wimp," replied Wally. "The bugger had even dropped to his knees and was pleading for his life and was trying to convince us that he was worth far more to us alive. After seeing me shoot the others, Martha was concerned that I might shoot him and suggested that we put him in a rowing boat and by the time he makes land we'd be gone. Carlos then begged to be put in a rowing boat but this lowlife had to meet his maker. He would have done the same and more to us. I squeezed the trigger and put a bullet between his eyes."

"No, you just shot the man in cold blood, Wally?" I looked shocked. "That's murder."

Wally laughed, "That was Martha's reaction too, except she became hysterical."

"How did my uncle react?" I asked.

"He understood where I was coming from but he could not have killed a man in cold blood. It had to be done and I did it gladly without any regrets. Anyhow," Wally continued, "it was late in the day so we cleared the deck and fed the tiger shark and settled down to an early night."

I cringed at the thought of the shark and its mates tearing through those bodies.

Wally picked up on my facial expression and laughed. "Well, it was the best way to destroy all the evidence. Tiger sharks will eat the lot, shoes and all."

"Gross!" I exclaimed.

"Your uncle agreed to take the overnight watch, though we didn't expect a search party until the next morning and by then we should be gone out of reach of even their faster vessels. My plan was for us to wake at dawn and use the first two hours to retrieve as much treasure as we could as I had found some valuable pieces. Unbeknown to me your uncle and Martha had other plans and at dawn, I woke to find that Carlo's boat and my crew had left. Nevertheless, I was determined to stick to my plan and managed with great difficulty on my own to retrieve two loads doing both the loading and pulling at the other end. I actually came away with a nice booty but regretfully had to leave the rest. No boat came that morning, though I suspect one was on its way. At one time an aeroplane flew low overhead but not long after I was well out of territorial waters. Anyhow that's my story."

"Now I understand why my uncle never wanted to tell this story. Interpol could have a warrant out for your arrest."

"I doubt it," replied Wally. "If there's no body then how can there be a murder? It was a silly place for them to go swimming when a hungry tiger shark was patrolling the area." He laughed again.

"You're quite heartless. Don't you feel any remorse at all?" I asked.

"None, it was tit for tat," he replied. "They would have done the same to us and I'm sure there would be many people on his island pleased that he's no longer there. I felt quite good about the whole thing but regret not throwing Carlos into the shark-infested waters with a bleeding wound and letting him experience the trauma of being eaten alive."

"So what happened to you after that with your business partner and girlfriend gone?"

"Oh, I returned to Australia, pottered around doing boat chartering work and diving for several years. I also mixed in with a bad crowd and got in rather too deep; lost a lot of my wealth gambling. Then one day the opportunity to get rich again arose when I was approached by this long-haired Kiwi bloke called Marty Johnson."

"Marty Johnson of Mr Asia fame?"

"Yes, that's the bloke. He was first called Mr Asia and had been making a lot of easy money importing drugs and supplying them to dealers in Australia and New Zealand. Marty was looking at the prospect of transporting heroin from Thailand to Australia and needed a boat. He and a group eventually bought their own — they called it the Brigadoon."

"You didn't," I said. "Dealing in drugs is so immoral."

"And why not?" Wally answered. "If people are stupid enough to put poisons into their bodies that's not my concern. As Marty said, it's just a business — supply and demand. Marty was doing very well for himself. I've never seen a man dressed so smartly in a three-piece suit. Anyhow, I carried out one or two runs for him and was rewarded handsomely and the operation seemed water-tight. Then this hard-core criminal feller, Terry Clark, muscled his way into Marty's business. Unlike Marty, he was a killer — a psychopath — known for his ruthlessness and intolerance to those who failed him. One day I received the word that Terry wanted to see me and had a job for me. Well, I didn't want to see him or have anything to do with him and fortunately had never met the man. I knew that I needed to disappear as quickly as possible if I valued my life. That night my boat slipped out of the harbour, was given a new name and I headed for a new life in Bali."

"And he was ruthless," I added. "My understanding is that many people in the operation, including Marty, ended up dead."

"Precisely why I left Australia and disappeared from circulation once he became involved," replied Wally. "Once you were involved with him there was only one way out and that's in a coffin. So your uncle's dead? I just can't believe it." Wally shook his head. "Such a waste of a good man."

"Yes, he got to the stage where there was nothing left for him in life. His death was a blessing."

"Was he survived by a wife and children?" Wally asked.

"No, I'm his only relative I'm afraid," I replied.

"Inherited the lot, Robbie?"

"Yes, but even considering the pirate's treasure, not much to show for it."

"Well, just remember there was Great Aunt Betty's legacy," Wally raucously laughed. That was so funny. Or don't you know about that?"

"Oh yes, Great Aunt Betty. I found out all about that," I replied.

"Your dad was a proud man and would never have accepted the money otherwise," explained Wally. "But after we found the pirate's treasure we had money to burn."

"So can you tell me the story about the pirate's treasure?" I asked as I put on my tee-shirt.

"Your uncle never told you?" Wally looked surprised. "It was the pirate's treasure which brought us to world fame as treasure-hunters and I thought everyone knew that story."

"No, Uncle was tight-lipped about all his adventures."

"Yes, I can understand that," replied Wally, "especially after our experience with the pirate's treasure."

"The pirate's treasure was our first adventure after both of us had served in the army overseas. We both had a taste for adventure and we were looking for a fourteenth-century Portuguese treasure ship which had sunk in the straits of Malacca when we became pursued by a gang of blood-thirsty men. Malacca Straits had a long history of piracy and it was still not uncommon to find pirates around there and the Indonesian Islands."

"So these were pirates?"

"Could have been," Wally laughed. "We managed to set sail but we knew it wouldn't be too long before they caught us as they had a faster boat as well as guns. We had rounded an island when their boat came into view. They started shooting at us at about the same time as we sighted several very small uninhabited islands ahead where we might lose them. Several had hilly terrain and vegetation in which we could hide. We passed between two islands then skirted around one of them well out of sight and sunk our boat in shallow water so it would not be found, but we could retrieve later. Your uncle and I pressed through the thick vegetation and it was only by accident that he stumbled over a large hole in the ground. He removed a few rocks and found it to be the entranceway into a large cave."

"The pirate's treasure?"

"Yes, I'm getting to that. We closed the hole up behind us and moved down into the cave and waited. It wasn't that dark as there was light breaking through cracks in the rock roof. Deeper into the cave your uncle spotted some old chests and I think you can guess the rest."

"What about the pursuers?"

"Funnily enough they never set foot, as far as we know, on the island. They probably thought that we might have gone to one of the bigger islands where there was more vegetation. I recall the ring you're wearing on your finger as being part of that treasure," Wally added, as he noticed it on my hand. "Did he give that to you?"

"Well, in a way, yes. He left me a key to a bank safe where he had some personal items and this was amongst them," I replied.

"Was my small red notebook amongst them?" asked Wally.

"Notebook?" I hesitated as I stood up from my beach chair. "There were several unusual items in the box and from memory, there could have been a notebook," I said, as I moved a safer distance from Wally.

"Well, I want it?" Wally roared. "It is mine. I thought at first that your uncle had sent you to return it."

"Could it have something to do with the General Grant?" I asked.

"General Grant? What about the General Grant?" Wally, who had started putting on his tee-shirt, stopped what he was doing.

"Well, there was talk that my uncle may have found the treasure of the General Grant."

"Over my dead body," replied a belligerent Wally, clenching his fist. "He wouldn't. Martha, your uncle and I had been planning the General Grant for months and there's no way he would or should have gone there without involving us — not if he valued his life."

"It was only a rumour." I wiped the sweat from my brow as I moved a little further away from an unpredictable Wally. "If he had, then where's the gold? Besides, who's to say that the survivors didn't take it? They were stranded on the island for eighteen months."

"Exactly, my thoughts too when Martha, your uncle and I discussed the venture." Wally wiped the sweat from his brow and had now calmed down. "I'd be most surprised if he went on an expedition behind my back looking for the General Grant. It was your uncle who thought such an expedition would be pointless after four salvage expeditions each involving a survivor of the General Grant. It was Martha who remained unpersuaded given the mountain of research she had done. As for those survivors on the island recovering the treasure, I think that would be highly unlikely, otherwise why would some of them want to return to that hell-hole? There's only one reason they'd want to and that's to recover the booty. Seriously, can you imagine the fifteen survivors on the island recovering the treasure and for the rest of the time until rescued living peacefully together? There would have been all-out warfare as each person disputed what was theirs. As it was, the scene almost turned ugly with only one woman amongst all those survivors."

"I guess you're right and that the gold would be the last thing on their minds when it all came down to survival on a desolate wind-swept sub-Antarctic island in just the clothes they were wearing at the time the ship went down," I sighed.

"Don't underestimate those people," said Wally. "Those people were quite resourceful, growing potatoes and even domesticating pigs and goats. They also made clothing and shoes."

"Out of what?" I looked surprised.

"Plenty of seals around," laughed Wally. "I hear that seal-skin clothing was the in fashion on the island at the time. My own opinion is that the survivors returned and recovered the gold."

"Oh!" I replied.

"Yes, a couple of years after the sinking, James Teer, a survivor, returned to the island with an expedition on the paddle tug, Southland. They claimed to have located the cave but couldn't enter because of bad weather."

"So, how long were they there for?" I asked.

"About a couple of weeks," replied Wally.

"Two weeks and they didn't find even one day or even just a couple of hours of calm weather to salvage the treasure? That's very hard to believe."

"You're onto it." Wally changed his position in his beach chair. "Apparently, in their first week the weather was stormy with high seas but in the second week the stormy weather had abated and they were able to send out a party of divers to the cave. This attempt was aborted when the wind picked up again and high seas returned. They then tried to get to the cave over land but this turned out to be a waste of time. In the end, the continuing bad weather and fuel shortages gave them no other option but to return to Invercargill."

"Sounds a convenient excuse" I commented. "Teer, having lived on those islands as a survivor, surely would have known if there was any land access to the cave."

"That's right," replied Wally. "Why would they even go there and why did Teer never return on another expedition? Perhaps just maybe they recovered the treasure and it was all hype about rough seas and a failed land attempt. Don't you think it unusual to be lured to the island with the thought of recovering the gold then to not want to return if the gold is still there?"

"Then two years later another survivor, a David Ashworth, set out on the Daphne expedition and that ended in disaster with only a couple from the expedition returning, the rest lost at sea. One year later a third survivor, a Cornelius Drew, set out on a vessel called the Flora. This was a very well-equipped ship with diving suits, blasting powder, ropes and much more. They spent three months on the island, which to me would suggest that, if the gold hadn't already been taken by the earlier expeditions then they would certainly have recovered it. Because of the rough seas, their plan was to cut a track up across the top to the west coast cliffs above the wreck site. They spent a month doing this and were going to build a work camp there then decided this was the wrong place and restarted building a track to a camp at Smith's Harbour. Can you believe that?"

"Hard to believe they'd do all that work then change their minds," I replied.

"It could, of course, account for the time getting into the hull of the General Grant and retrieving the gold," suggested Wally. "They were planning on blowing up the roof of the cave to block it then they wouldn't have to worry about the sea."

"How deep was the water in the cave?" I asked.

"Eighteen fathoms but it got deeper at the mouth."

"So did they?"

"No, somebody didn't like the idea as it could bury the wreck and it was hardly enough rock to block the cave from the sea." Wally laughed. "One of the men, not keen on the idea, threw the explosives into the sea and that was the end of that. Then they put men over the cliffs on ropes but claimed to have only found pieces of wreckage."

"Sure!" I laughed. "I think I can see where you're coming from. These expeditions were led by survivors who knew the island, knew the cave where the wreck lay, where the gold was stored and, in Drew's case, given three months. With all that equipment would have recovered the treasure."

"Oh, and Cornelius Drew returned with another expedition a year later, found the cave, located the wreck but due to rough weather abandoned the salvage."

"Did he return?" I asked.

"No, my opinion, which I expressed to your uncle and Martha at the time, is that he got what he was looking for and we'd be wasting our time looking for the gold. But, just in case, if you hear anything more about the General Grant then keep me informed, and I want that notebook back, it's mine. Do you hear?" Wally started to get agitated again.

"I will have a look amongst my uncle's personal belongings," I promised, as I left the old man on his beach chair and returned to the hotel.

Chapter 16

"If shopping doesn't make you happy, then you're in the wrong shop."

Anonymous

Back at the hotel Mary was in the bedroom repacking her suitcase.

"So Wally was OK then?" Mary asked. "I could have told you there was nothing to worry about. Fancy worrying about being beaten up by an eighty-year-old man," Mary laughed as she continued putting clothes into her suitcase. "Really!"

"Maybe eighty plus but you should have seen him; he was built like a gorilla," I replied.

"Sure," Mary laughed again. "Pull the other one. Did he have his walking stick with him?"

"Now how are we going to get all of this back to New Zealand?" I growled, having just noticed Mary's new purchases spread across the bed. I frowned at the thought of the airline weight restrictions.

"No problem," Mary replied. "We'll take it back on the plane with us of course."

"No problem, Mary! You obviously don't understand that this is how airlines make their money, charging for excess baggage. We have a maximum of seven kilograms each." I threw my hands up in despair.

"Plus check-in luggage," replied Mary. "Nobody flies to Bali with just carry-on luggage."

"I know, I know, it's all my mistake Mary, but it just isn't worth paying now for check-in luggage. It's going to cost more for this than what you'll save on your purchases. It costs something ridiculous like $100 plus per 20 kilograms."

"Well, there you go; it's all paid for then," said Mary. "I bought a large check-in suitcase for $100 less than what you'd pay in New Zealand. Besides your cheaper airfare was only because there was no check-in luggage, so it's not as if we're paying business class by adding check-in luggage."

"I'm going down to the swimming pool," I said, as I left the room in a huff.

The pool seemed to be quite popular with hotel guests sunbathing on loungers under a hot blazing sun and others swimming and chilling out. I found an empty lounger in the shade and stretched out. What with the humidity, Mary's spending addiction and Wally's aggressive stance, the day had been emotionally draining and I was none the wiser concerning the General Grant, except for the fact that it had been on my uncle's radar. Tomorrow, I would try to catch up with Wally again and arrange the return of his notebook as well as seek answers to the revolver and passports in my uncle's safety deposit box. I sat for half an hour or so blobbing out on the lounger in thought before returning to our hotel room.

In my absence, Mary had once again been busy and had planned shopping at Bali Collection for the next day.

"No, tomorrow morning I will need to catch up again with Wally," I told her. "That was the main purpose of coming to Bali."

"Oh well, I was thinking we could buy lunch there, but we can do without lunch given the amount of food you've been stuffing away each breakfast." Mary was not at all upset and had been thinking that it would be nice spending a morning or two in the pool anyway. "There will be other days for shopping," she added.

And that was exactly my fear given her shopping addiction. This needed to be addressed as I left the room for the hotel lobby to book a few sight-seeing tours to occupy the remainder of our Bali holiday.

The next morning I enquired at the reception to Wally's whereabouts. They suggested that I might find him back down on the beach, where he liked to hang out. I crossed the road and headed for the alleyway past two well-built Indonesian men who were smoking outside the Travel Lodge Hotel. They gave me more than a cursory glance which reminded me that I shouldn't be flashing that Rolex on my wrist. I guess that I should have heeded Wally's warning but I'd become quite attached to my uncle's watch and by then I had entered the alleyway. My fears of being assaulted and robbed now became very real as I had noticed that the two men had started to follow me and the only way out of the alleyway was now at the beach end. Once again anxiety took centre stage and my heart-rate suddenly trebled. I quickened my pace to almost a run as the two men seemed to be drawing closer. I was now drawing a heavy sweat given the high humidity but, fortunately, the other end of the alleyway was in sight. To my relief, I reached the beach. It was deserted. Wally wasn't there and I guess that an eighty-year-old wouldn't have been of much assistance anyhow had I been assaulted. I now had no alternative but to continue along a path at the top of the beach which tracked the shoreline. This formed a dividing line between the beach and the hotels fronting onto to it. I quickly glanced back and sure enough, the two men coming out of the alleyway were now taking the same path and heading in my direction. Further along the path, I found an exit leaving the beach but unfortunately down another alleyway. I reluctantly and hurriedly took this and was pleased when it eventually widened out into a market area. Here there were three rows of tented stalls selling mostly clothing. I entered one of the stalls, moving well inside the tent and out of sight. A minute or two later I watched as the two men briskly passed by.

"Well, which tee-shirt do you want?" the lady in the stall asked. She had been waiting for me to make up my mind and hadn't realised the real reason for my entering her tent. I guess that this was the price I had to pay for stepping on her turf but she had, in a sense, come to my rescue. I quickly looked for a few seconds and decided on one that said Bali, Bali.

"Good choice," said the lady, removing it from a hanger. Then we began to barter on the price. There were no other customers at the stalls and I felt sorry for these people. They were poor and this was their livelihood, so I didn't barter too hard and gave her a good price.

The stalls were just off the road so I felt safe and was able to return along the footpath to my hotel.

"Followed?" Mary looked at me disbelievingly. "I certainly hope that you're not going to get all paranoid at Bali Collection this afternoon. What nonsense."

Mary dismissed my story as another case of anxiety, this time brought on by the sheer coincidence that the men happened to just be walking in the same direction.

That afternoon we crossed the road from the hotel, where the two men had been standing earlier in the day, and we caught the free bus to Bali Collection. The place was bigger than I envisaged with many single-storey shops spread over a large area of land. It was a place designed for tourists and the prices didn't look any cheaper than what we'd pay in our own country. Obviously, they were tourist prices.

"Scratch and win. Would you like to win free hotel accommodation in Vietnam?" asked a man, approaching Mary.

"Vietnam? I'd love to, I've heard that it's great shopping there," replied Mary excitedly.

My heart raced at the thought that Bali may just be the start to Mary's shopping adventures with Vietnam and Thailand to follow.

"No, it's a time-share, Mary," I whispered, dragging her away by the arm. "I certainly don't want to be wasting some of my inheritance on a one week's holiday home and as well, annual management fees for the rest of our lives. Do you really want to be rushed off to their offices to spend the rest of the day listening to some hard-sell salesman, Mary?"

"No thank you," replied Mary to the man, as she now realised what was behind the offer and more importantly the fact that she'd miss her shopping.

For me, the rest of the afternoon seemed to drag on one boring hour after another as we looked through nearly every shop — the worst being clothing and women's wear. At one point I stood in trepidation as Mary spent some time eying up some beautiful wooden carvings which would certainly adorn our shelves at home but also collect the dust. Fortunately, she moved on after commenting, "The prices here are much higher than Hardy's."

I was quick to agree with her even though I had never been to Hardy's.

Coming out of a shop I noticed a man across the road. He seemed to be taking a particular interest in us even though he was trying to be inconspicuous, occasionally looking down at a brochure. I recognised him at once as one of the men who had followed me through the alleyway.

"Mary, we're being followed," I said. "It's the same man."

"Not again," replied a disbelieving Mary.

"We need to lose him," I replied, "and this is a good time to head back for the next bus which will be leaving shortly."

"Yes, we could make our way back now, I think I'm pretty much done here." Mary led the way back past shops, which for me brought back painful memories, towards the bus stop.

"Quick, duck in here, we're still being followed." I pulled Mary into a department store, Mary almost dropping her purchases in the process.

"Don't be so silly, Mr Anxiety. I've got some fragile things in this bag and you nearly made me drop it. Anyhow, I thought that you didn't like shopping." she replied. "Most unlike you to drag me into a shop."

I tried to hurry her through the store to another entrance where we managed to exit.

"You know I don't like to say this but I think that you may be right and we are being followed," she said, as she had spotted a man running into the department store just as we were leaving.

But now Mary was also running instead of being dragged. From there we turned down several other roads, within the Bali Collection shopping area, before reaching the bus stop. Instead of going to the bus stop, I pulled Mary into the Nike store where we wouldn't be seen.

"Good to see that you're finally doing something about your appearance," Mary teased. She leapt at the opportunity to hunt around and select from some casual shoes on sale. "Here try these on, they seem to be a good price and will look very smart on you."

"Mary, I brought you in here as we can see from here when our bus arrives. I certainly didn't come in here to buy shoes."

But before I could do anything, the salesman had grabbed the opportunity and was preparing the shoe for me to try on.

"Now that's a good fit and looks great," said Mary.

"Perfect, would you like it wrapped?" asked the salesman.

"Our bus," I said, looking out the window.

"We have time," replied Mary, as she passed over the money and waited for the shoes.

I guess I'll have to get to like these shoes, I thought, as we left and found a seat on the bus. It appeared that we had lost the man who had been following.

"As Wally told you, flashing around that Rolex was always going to get us into trouble," Mary said, as we travelled back to the hotel.

It was a comforting thought to know that the shopping was now behind us and our remaining time would be spent on organised tours over the island. In particular, I was looking forward to the buffet lunches provided on each tour. But as Robbie Burns said in one of his poems, "The best-laid schemes of mice and men don't always go to plan." I had never counted on street markets at nearly every stop on each tour and of course, Mary was keen to find a few more bargains. The prices here were a lot cheaper than Bali Collection and Hardy's. Now she seemed to be buying more than ever, somewhat worrying given that she only had an extra twenty-kilogram allowance and that looked to have been already reached.

Over the remaining days, I continued to feel like I was under surveillance. The spies seemed to be everywhere: a taxi driver in the hotel lobby, a customer at a restaurant and even people on some tours. "It's probably your Rolex," Mary suggested. "More-so since you had it cleaned up and it looks brand new. It does look fabulous, but there again it could be those new shoes drawing the unwanted attention." She laughed as she didn't take me seriously. "You seem to have taken a shine to them. I just hope that you don't wear them out before we get back home."

I was pleased when our holiday ended and we were returning on the plane with no excess to pay on Mary's baggage.

Chapter 17

"Where we love is home-home that our feet may leave,

but not our hearts."

Oliver Wendell Holmes

"Home sweet home," said Mary as we walked in through the doorway. "I thought you only had carry-on luggage," Harry commented, smirking as I carried in Mary's large suitcase.

"Don't go there, Harry," I warned glaring in his direction. "Not a popular subject."

"Well the check-in suitcase was such a bargain, Harry," replied Mary, grinning. "It would certainly be a waste if we didn't use it again. I hear that Thailand has cheap hotels, cheap shopping and lots of nice beaches, dear," Mary added, turning towards me with a smile.

I felt a lump in my throat develop at the thought of having to endure another long torturous journey cooped up in an aeroplane seat for hours in order to visit another overcrowded Third World country. We didn't need another shopping expedition and at our ages the additional clutter of souvenirs gathering dust on our shelves. But then life must get boring for Mary stuck inside and missing all the excitement of mending fences and moving sheep and cattle to different paddocks, though at times she does help. I put down the suitcases where no one would trip over them and out of sight as I didn't need a reminder of the shopping expedition. It was ironic that I'd been given the job of carrying the big suitcase when I was the one never in favour of taking check-in luggage.

"Here," said Mary, who had been sorting through a week's mail that had accumulated in our absence. She handed me a letter. "It's from your uncle's solicitor." Mary watched as I opened the letter.

"Looks like a cheque!" I exclaimed as I excitedly removed the contents of the envelope. "The rogues! My uncle's solicitor and accountant's fees come to almost ten grand."

"They certainly know how to charge," replied Mary. "They say that death attracts vultures. I did tell you to leave the solicitor to do all the talking as they're charging you for their time. I expect you expounded your theory on your uncle and the General Grant?"

"It was discussed but I can assure you that the solicitor did most of the talking," I replied.

"Sure." Mary wasn't convinced.

"Good, I can now buy my new Massey Ferguson tractor. I'm looking forward to having a brand new one and one with a three-point hydraulic controlled linkage. I can't wait to use it." I was very excited about having all this money now at our disposal.

"And I can finally get a new kitchen," added a hopeful Mary. "I'll have a double oven and two or three power stations. Self-closing drawers would also be handy given that you're always leaving them open."

"Yes, of course, you can," I replied. "I also need a new vehicle."

"Well, don't get anything like a Merc, Audi or Beamer," advised Mary, "or you'll upset Colin."

"No, it'll be a new ute. Our old one has been no end of trouble and I don't have the mechanical skills to keep fixing it, Mary. It's still leaking oil and the first gear is shot."

"And you talk about me going on a shopping frenzy," commented Mary. "There you go, this one takes the cake. You get a bit of money in your hands and you're away on a spending spree. I think there might even be enough left for a trip to Thailand."

"It's a case of needing to replace worn-out assets," I replied. "These assets generate our income just in case you hadn't noticed, but you're most welcome to your kitchen and if you like you can have it in colours to match your new suitcase."

"Well, that's so kind of you to let me have a small portion," replied Mary. "It would be nice to update my car as well."

"Of course you can," I replied. "I'm tired of trying to fix that vehicle."

"Talking about Colin, I guess he will expect me to update him on events, although I'm sure he will be very jealous when I drive my new ute to town. Our relationship was good when I was a poor farmer with a rusty old ute and, initially, our meetings were therapeutic given all my anxiety over the General Grant."

"Tell me about it," interrupted Mary.

"But now he seems to be less friendly and he's always telling me what to do, Mary."

"Well, he's right, just like the pastor was in telling you not to share with others about the General Grant. Now, after all this sharing and worrying, you're starting to realise that this was one salvage operation your uncle was never involved in," replied Mary. "Both your uncle's partners have confirmed that they know nothing about the General Grant and that should be more than enough to persuade anyone."

"Not quite true, Mary. Wally said that they had looked into an expedition into searching for the wreck. He was just upset at the thought that my uncle would have excluded him from this salvage operation after the input both he and Martha had."

"He also told you that they both agreed to abandon the idea after concluding that one of the survivor-led expeditions would have recovered it," added Mary, "and I think that he's right."

"Yes, I guess you're right," I sighed. "There have been many salvage attempts; a number of these by the actual survivors. They would have to know where the wreck lay."

"Colin seems to have an axe to grind and I think you're right, he will be jealous," said Mary. "He should be grateful that he has a good job and I understand a wife, though I've never met her."

Unlike Colin, I had never seen the underbelly of our society and had little idea of how dangerous my situation could become. I had been followed in Bali, but that was more likely a result of my flashing the Rolex watch, rather than the prospect of sitting on millions of dollars of gold bars. Colin, as usual, wanted to know everything when we met and this time I decided not to tell him about my meeting with my uncle's old partner.

"The world is not a level playing field," commented Colin, when he saw me pull up outside Traffers in a new ute just after returning from a holiday in Bali. Word had already gotten around town so he had heard also about my new tractor purchase. "Ah, so you found the gold and you're now cashing it in?"

"What gold, Colin? I've been spending my inheritance money. The IRD must be satisfied as the solicitor sent me a cheque while I was away. But you're right, the solicitor and accountant are both rogues with their whopping fees." I filled my glass.

"Well, we can agree on that." Colin put down his glass. "It's criminal what they get away with Robbie, but you're not being totally honest with me.

You're spending more than the pittance you told me that you were disappointed in receiving. Just in my head, I'm calculating several hundred thousand on just what I know you've purchased so far. Then we have your gold Rolex watch that looks to me to be brand new and not the cheap Asian imitation you were flashing around before. So you say it was in the deposit box, which I doubt very much. Did the deposit box ever exist or was it a storage unit where the gold was stashed?"

"Same watch, Colin, but just cleaned up," I replied. "I took advantage of the cheap labour and had it cleaned in Bali," I replied.

"Sure! You haven't changed and always did have an answer for everything. Just remember that you need a friend in the police force as this gold of yours has attracted a lot of criminal interest in our otherwise peaceful town. We need to move it to a safe place."

"Oh, you mean Jack?" I asked.

"No, not just him, but he's still hanging around town. I understand he's working on another farm, which begs the question, why and what interest does he have in Gore? Are you sure you don't want to lay a complaint? These people are better locked away rather than upsetting the community and wasting our time. It's so much easier to do once they have a criminal record."

"Lock him up for what?" I asked. "It seems that whenever there's a crime the first people to be suspected are those with a criminal record, the destitute, and the defenceless. We don't know who pulled up the floorboards and if the steer was stolen or just keeled over. The fact that Jack is having to find a meal and freeboard suggest that he's got enough to deal with. I'd have him back any day if he chose to return because he's a good, skilled worker."

"He could also be staking out a job that might involve your gold. Just be mindful that he hasn't left town and he may very well have accomplices here."

"Like the pastor?" I sniggered.

"Not just the pastor," replied Colin. "Now that you're throwing around money you may find that things start to get hot and it won't just be me asking where you have your gold stored."

"But as I said, I don't have the gold and from all my investigations I'm now convinced that my uncle never found it. Oh yes, he knew about the gold and the adventure was on his to-do list but I'm now pretty sure that it never happened." I gulped down what was left in my glass of beer. "The fact is that there were many salvage attempts involving the survivors of the General Grant and they had the equipment and time to recover the treasure."

"I don't believe you, and there are other criminals here I recognised from Auckland as well," added Colin.

"Others?"

"Hardened criminals," clarified Colin. "Now what would have drawn them to Gore of all places, Robbie? These people don't just travel the length of New Zealand to have a picnic. Anyhow, it's your gold to do what you like with, just don't say I didn't warn you and support you as a friend. Changing the subject, did you have a nice holiday in Bali?"

"Not my thing at all," I replied. "I can't understand why people want to leave our beautiful country to spend time somewhere else. What can an overcrowded Third World country offer apart from cheap hotels, cheap food and cheap shopping?" My stomach felt uncomfortable at the thought of having wasted a day visiting shops and stalls.

"I would gladly have made the trip if I had the money," replied Colin, "but after the bank has collected their share from my wages and I've paid the rates, electricity and groceries and my wife has dipped in as well, there's usually only enough left for a couple of beers."

That night I sat down with my other son who was home from Otago University and we tried to decode the red notebook, but to no avail.

"Have you heard of the enigma code?" asked my second son, James.

"No," I replied.

"It was the code the Germans used during the war and was finally cracked by the British. The fact is that codes can be incredibly difficult to crack and nowadays making them with computers pretty much impossible."

Who was my uncle really? It was a mystery in itself that he or somebody else had gone to so much trouble to encode but to hide what? I decided that night that I would return the notebook to Wally as it was really of no use to me coded. Perhaps returning it was what my uncle had always intended and the real reason he wanted me to visit Wally. But if it was that important to Wally then he'd be in touch and anyway I was content having just the inheritance. The gold of the General Grant, if it existed, would, of course, be more than a bonus but it could also end up being an encumbrance. For instance, Mary would want her shopping trip to Thailand, then probably Vietnam, Cambodia and so forth annually. I guess I could do a lot of good with the money, help the pastor out and those in need, but the downside is that charity organisations seldom accept just a one-off donation and return with their other hand held out. While it's nice to dream about all that gold, the millions of dollars' worth of gold bars, the fact was that there would have been little gold if any left for my uncle after all those salvage operations in the nineteenth century. Yet, at my uncle's funeral, the Auckland diver suggested to the contrary. What information did he have to convince me otherwise, that my uncle had found the gold of the General Grant?

Chapter 18

"We must learn who is gold, and who is gold plated."

Anonymous

My plane touched down at Auckland and I made my way out to the buses and taxis and waited for the free shuttle to my hotel in Mangere. It was nice to know that this was free, as Auckland, similarly to other big cities worldwide, was known as being expensive for transport and hotels. Compared to the Bali Ibis my hotel was quite basic and was one of the cheapest I could find, but was more than adequate for a one night stay. This time I'd decided to stay overnight, given my jam-packed agenda of visiting both the diver and the bank. At the hotel, they gave me directions to the Mangere town centre where I could catch a bus to the inner city. Based on these directions I locked up my hotel room and strode off through the neighbourhood towards the town centre. It wasn't too long before I had reached it and not long after that before I was off to town on a bus.

As a rural lad, riding in a bus down suburban streets was a new experience. Being elevated so much higher one seemed to see so much more of the real world than from a car. I was surprised as we passed through the first suburbs to see how close houses were to each other and the state and size of the houses. Living in the country our next-door neighbour lived kilometres away. Here, in contrast, each house seemed to be in the face of the next and many were small plain wooden houses with tin roofs and in need of a coat of paint. I guessed that this must be one of the poorer parts of the city where the houses are either rented or the owners cannot afford the maintenance. In all fairness, many of these people might not have the time because they could be holding down more than one job. Auckland was, after all, an expensive place to live.

Once in the centre of Auckland I carved my way down several streets, now quite confidently having been to the bank previously. Nervously I approached the bank with my uncle's notebook tucked securely in my hand. Again I was led into Fort Knox by the well-dressed gentleman where I followed the required protocol before being left in the privacy of the viewing area. I paused for a moment, inhaling several deep breaths before turning the key. I slowly raised the lid. It was not a pretty sight, one that I had wanted to forget, but I knew that the gun and passports wouldn't just miraculously disappear. Their presence was still weighing on my mind as they contradicted nearly everything I had believed about my uncle. I quickly placed the notebook into the box, then slammed the lid shut, securing it forever I hoped. For now, the notebook was safe and the gun and passports could be pushed to the back of my mind once again. I returned the box to the safe, giving a sigh of relief, but still left with a nasty taste in my mouth. Now I was more eager than ever to learn just who my uncle was. I quickly retraced my steps to the bus depot. I needed now more than anything to meet up with the diver, Andrew Parker, to have that reassurance that my uncle was not a bad guy and finally, I should also get more answers to my questions about the General Grant.

Andrew Parker lived in a suburb close to the central city, called Parnell. Travelling on the bus through this suburb I could not help but notice the difference in housing compared to some of the suburbs I had passed through in South Auckland. Andrew was obviously a wealthy man as I knew house prices in Auckland were incredibly high and in this area would be well over a million or two. His house was a well-maintained two-story house with a late model BMW parked outside on his concrete driveway. His front lawn looked to be meticulously manicured where not one ugly dandelion or other weed dared show its head. I had often wondered how people managed to produce such weed-free lawns when the sparrows, blackbirds and thrushes persistently sowed unwanted seeds.

I rang the doorbell which pleasantly chimed to Beethoven's 5th.

The door opened slowly and the same tall grey-headed man that I had met at the funeral appeared.

"Welcome to sunny Auckland, Robert." Andrew extended his hand to shake and invited me into his warm house.

"What a nice house," I commented.

It was an older house with a very slight musty smell but the varnished interior looked well-maintained and, like the lawns, was stunning.

"I guess this is a nice break for you getting away from the cold south."

"Yes," I replied.

"It was sad that your uncle passed away as we got on quite well. He will certainly be missed."

"Thank you, yes he will, and it is good to catch up with all his acquaintances as these days I'm learning just how little I knew about him. This weather is a nice change as it has been pretty cold recently down south. Quite frustrating losing so many days on the farm to bad weather when I have busy times ahead with lambing and calving. I know people in Auckland find it hard to believe, but we can get some pretty hot days down south as well."

"Come through and take a seat." Andrew led me into a spacious lounge area to a comfortable expensive leather lounge suite. "Coffee?"

"Yes, please but no sugar. Mary, my wife, says that people my age are more likely to end up with type two diabetes." I took a seat on one of the comfortable chairs.

"It's not just sugar," commented the diver. "We need to reduce our carbohydrate intake as we eat too much food in the western world and living on a farm I guess you probably eat too much meat."

"You've got a very nice house and location," I commented as I noted how each room was tastefully colour coordinated and spotlessly tidy, devoid of that cluttered family house look.

"Thank you, we rather like it ourselves. It's a nice quiet location and we've been here nearly forty years," he smiled. "Even then it cost us a fortune as houses do in Auckland. I was able to purchase this and my sailing boat using my share from the proceeds of the General Grant."

"Sorry?" I stared at the diver in shock. "Are you telling me that the story about recovering the General Grant's treasure is really true, that you and my uncle recovered the gold?"

"Why, of course," replied Andrew. "Surely, you must be aware that most of the millions you inherited came from the General Grant, though I understand that your uncle was very wealthy from other successful expeditions."

"What millions? Gregory Brown told the IRD when they interviewed us about my uncle's estate that a General Grant salvage operation never happened." I waited for Andrew's reaction.

"The IRD?" Andrew looked a little concerned. "Are they involved?"

"Not now, I understand that the investigation has now been completed."

"Oh good." Andrew looked relieved. "Gregory lied, of course, but that's to be expected. He's a con-man and habitual liar. He'd have been more at home in politics. Goodness me, an IRD investigation after all these years, that sounds draconian. What on earth would have triggered an investigation?"

"An anonymous source the accountant thinks," I replied.

"Yes, I'd imagine an investigation wouldn't get too far; not with Gregory having such powerful friends in high places," said the diver. "I don't think that the IRD will be any threat, not now after all these years, but it's interesting that they asked and why? So you've probably concluded by now that Gregory is not one to be trusted. I found this out following our expedition. Once you get your inheritance he will be around like a shot wanting to invest if for you. He's quite good at investing other people's money and losing it. You probably won't be aware but your uncle and Gregory cheated me out of millions of dollars' worth of other gold which would come in quite handy now as I head towards retirement."

"Other gold?"

"Yes," replied Andrew. "There was other gold additional to the gold bars in the shipwreck and I believe that your uncle and Gregory returned to the Auckland Islands to recover it. It would be nice to have my share as property prices in Auckland continue to rise steeply. Amazingly, this house is now worth over $2 million."

"You've done very well then," I replied. "You must be pleased that your wealth has increased significantly."

"Pleased? Not really, unless I was thinking of selling and then I'd still have to buy on the same market. When the value goes up so also do the rates and insurance. Now how are we supposed to pay all these expenses with a paltry state pension? This is my home, the home in which we raised our children, and I certainly don't want to be forced into selling it. It's alright for you farmers with your large land areas and low rural rates."

I looked at Andrew, quite surprised. It seemed that with all of the over-reaction to climate change that farmers had now become the bad-guys. Everyone these days seemed to find something negative to say about farmers.

Andrew laughed. "You don't have to take the post as well."

"Sorry?"

"Well, you looked like you'd taken offence, you know—a fence. I didn't mean my comment in a provocative way, my friend."

"Yeah, right," I replied.

"And they say there's no such thing as a double positive." Andrew laughed again. "You're a bit of a character just like your uncle. He was a nice man and I trusted him. But I was shocked to have found out sometime later that no sooner had we returned to the mainland to off-load our booty from the General Grant that Gregory and your uncle returned to recover the other gold. Now more than ever I need my share of this other gold."

"Well, I'm sorry to say that I don't have any gold and the inheritance I did receive was substantially less than what I would have expected from a man who found a pirate's treasure, let alone the General Grant."

"Were you not the sole beneficiary, then?" asked the diver, somewhat puzzled.

"Yes, I was," I replied. "Tell me, why are the property prices so high in Auckland?"

"Well, it all boils down to supply and demand," replied Andrew. "Our government wants to bring in all these immigrants and naturally because we have the best climate in the country most want to live in Auckland. This stretches our infrastructure, meaning that Auckland residents are not only left with a larger housing shortage but also higher rates to pay for more roads, improved water supply, sewerage disposal and so forth. Our water supply is no longer sufficient so we now have to draw it from the Waikato River. Your uncle had strong views on immigration, having seen the resulting problems overseas."

"So my uncle held strong views on how the world should be run?"

"He certainly did," the diver sniggered. "The world would be a different place had he been in charge."

"Was my uncle a bad guy, maybe a criminal?" I suggested.

"Now who told you that rubbish? No, not at all," laughed Andrew. "What a question, but I guess that anybody who is a partner of Gregory must fall under that suspicion. I can say that he was a bit of an enigma though, as he wasn't the stereotype who'd be out diving for shipwrecks and treasure."

"Oh, he wasn't?" I looked surprised as my uncle was renowned as being a treasure-hunter.

"Yes, I know what you're thinking and I know about all his history," said Andrew, who was picking up on my contorted facial expressions. "No, he was well outside his comfort zone in a diver's suit. So tell me how much do you know about the General Grant?"

"My uncle used to tell me the story frequently but he was a bit short on facts," I replied. "He was never one to disclose secrets, not even on his death bed."

"Yes, that was your uncle as I also knew him. So, let me start with the boat. The General Grant as you may have picked up on from its name was built in America and named after a famous American Civil War general. She was built of oak and pine, weighed 1,000 ton but was certainly not the fastest of vessels. They called her a clipper but she was more a cargo boat carrying three masts and two deckhouses for passengers. Now we get to the interesting bit regarding the passengers. Many of the passengers were Australian gold miners returning to England and they were carrying their fortunes in gold dust, coins, bars and nuggets because they had no trust in the banks."

"Who does?" I replied. "They pay pathetic interest on your money then they try and claw all that back in bank fees."

"Exactly," Andrew agreed. "The point I want to make here is that the cargo not only included the reported 73 kilograms of gold bars plus more but also 30 tons of spelter."

"So what's spelter, Andrew?"

"Now that's a very good question," replied the diver. "Why would they include it in the cargo to England when it's only a cheap yellow metal used to make decorative items? Could it have been gold? Now think about it, Robert, 70 tons is massive and there are many gold miner passengers on board returning to live in England. Obviously, because of the weight, they can't carry all their gold from years of mining on them in person, and these people didn't trust the banks for them to leave it behind. Then there was the case of the clipper Madagascar that went missing sixteen years before with millions worth of gold on board. It was never found."

"The Madagascar?" I looked perplexed.

"Yes, Robert, the Madagascar. It was returning from Melbourne to England in 1853 through the Southern Ocean and was carrying two tons of gold. What happened to the clipper is widely open to speculation, especially since it had pretty much a new crew. Most of the original crew from the journey to Melbourne left to make their fortune in the Victorian gold rush. Before the ship left Melbourne three of the people on board were arrested and removed by the police; one had been involved in a serious robbery. It certainly raises the question as to whether other criminals were on board and whether it may have been hijacked. So you can see that after the Madagascar mystery the miners on the General Grant would certainly not want their gold listed as gold. Listing it as spelter was a far safer alternative."

"But we don't know that for a fact."

"No, we don't, but they're hardly going to leave their gold behind in Australia are they, Robert?"

"There's a lot of ifs and buts, Andrew. It might just have been what it was listed as, spelter."

"Robert, these were very nervous people protective of their gold. One of the passengers, James Teer, carried 300 gold guineas in a body belt around his waist and he was not the only one carrying some amount of gold on them, but there's a limit to how much as gold is very heavy. If the gold is in an alluvial form then it needs to be bagged. Anyhow, after the survivors were rescued and returned to Australia, Teer joined an expedition as the guide and they set out in a steam tug called Southland to return to the wreck and recover the gold. But the seas around the Auckland Island are exposed to the Roaring Forties and due to rough seas and with fuel running low they returned to New Zealand empty-handed."

"Roaring Forties?"

"Yes, the strong westerly winds between the latitudes of 40 and 50 degrees. After that, Teer gave up on the treasure hunt. In 1870 another ship, a topsail schooner called Daphne, set out with David Ashworth, another survivor of the General Grant, as their guide. This time they made it and even to the cave where the ship had sunk."

"Well then, with Ashworth in the party he would know exactly where the ship went down, the position of the wreck and the gold cargo," I commented.

"Exactly, you're onto it, Robert. This now takes me to another story of how we found the treasure."

"Wait a minute, that doesn't make sense as they would surely have taken the treasure," I said.

"That's right, so you need to bear with me and follow the rest of the story, Robert. Those on board the Daphne comprised: Captain Wallace, David Ashworth, a diver, a cabin boy and five others. The cabin boy was my grandfather and my story is his story."

"Your grandfather?"

"Yes. Anyhow after the Daphne arrived at the Auckland Islands it set up anchor until they struck a calm day. They chose a more sheltered spot so the Daphne wouldn't meet the same fate as the General Grant and other ships. Early the next morning the captain and six men set off in three large boats to spread the weight of the gold and bring it all back in one trip. They knew the calm weather wouldn't last long and there might be only a small window of opportunity. Another seaman and the ship's cook followed in the Daphne's dingy so they knew where they had gone just in case the salvage operation ran into problems. The party rowed around the north-west cape where Ashworth was able to identify the cave. With Ashworth as a guide, they found the wreck quite quickly and initially the diver brought up small items like gold coins together with some gold bars and they packed what they could in the dingy and sent it on its way. The dingy, now riding low in the water, could only support the cook's weight and he returned solo to the Daphne with these spoils. Later that day, before the others returned with the rest of the treasure, a fierce storm blew up and all the cabin boy (my grandfather) and the cook could do was to ride out the turbulent waters. After the sea had settled the cook suggested that they needed to check on the salvage operation. The cook had presumed that the party probably had taken shelter in the cave from the perilous waters. They set out for the cave and were off the northern coast when they found pieces of boat and oars floating in the water but there were no bodies. They were about to leave when the cabin boy spotted a head bobbing up in the water. It was their diver, who, through his breathing and swimming skills, had managed to defy death. But the poor man was close to drowning and it wasn't until after spewing up buckets of seawater that he was able to explain how they had loaded all the boats with the treasure and were returning in a convoy when from out of nowhere this violent storm arose. They had little chance as the boats with the weight of the gold were riding low in the water and all aboard were most reluctant to jettison any of it. He was able to identify the spot the boats capsized using the cliff structure of the coastline as a marker. They returned to the Daphne and the cook and seaman were able to sketch a map setting out the area where the treasure was now located. That night the seaman died."

"Died?" I looked surprised.

"Not at all uncommon, Robert" replied Andrew. "People who have almost drowned can die later. It probably requires twenty-four hours before you can be taken off the critical list."

"Anyhow the cook and my grandfather threw him overboard to be with his shipmates. That's the way he would have liked it. My grandfather at the time might have been a cabin boy but was smart enough to realise that he wouldn't get any of the gold now in the cook's possession. While the cook was preparing the meal the next day my uncle slipped surreptitiously into the captain's cabin, copied the map and grabbed some handfuls of gold coins and managed to hide these away amongst his belongings. The cook never found out and together they managed to sail the boat back to Bluff, New Zealand, where a search party was raised to search for the missing sailors. Several boats went out to the Auckland Islands but the missing seamen were never found. What happened to the cook remains a mystery but one can rest assured that he ended up a wealthy man and needn't put his life at risk ever again. As a child, my grandfather made use of his good fortune and used the gold to get a good education and in turn a well-paid job. He too, well aware of the dangerous conditions, never returned in search of the treasure but he retained the hand-drawn sketch of its location which ended up in my hands."

"So the Daphne was in 1870?" I reiterated. "And the General Grant sank in 1866?"

"Yes, that's right," Andrew replied. "And after this failed attempt where Ashworth and others lost their lives the interest in a treasure hunt tended to fade as people realised just how dangerous it was around the Auckland Islands. In 1876 another General Grant survivor—a Cornelius Drew, accompanied the crew of the schooner Flora and they found the cave..."

"Which they would if he was a survivor," I interjected.

"... yes, but bad weather prevented them in their salvage attempts and food shortages ended their hope," continued Andrew. "The next attempt to salvage the treasure where a diver entered the cave was a whole fifty years later and he found nothing. If there had been any remaining bags of spelter or should I say gold, then the bags would have disintegrated and the contents spilt over the seafloor."

"Then the same would be true of those bags retrieved by the Daphne wouldn't they if they were in the water for four years?" I asked.

"Maybe, but the salvage crew would have planned for this and would have transferred the contents to much sturdier bags before hoisting them up onto their boats. Remember, they had one of the surviving passengers with them who undoubtedly would have had a good knowledge about the cargo and what the Daphne expedition would need for the salvage. Fifty years later when the next known treasure-hunters appeared on the scene and searched the seafloor there was no treasure."

"You took it?"

"Too right. Would you like another coffee, Robert, then I'll tell you our story?"

Andrew went away, bringing back two cups of coffee while I made myself comfortable. The whole General Grant story had been a roller-coaster ride and now it would seem that the story was true, but what happened to the gold then? Could the solicitor or accountant have embezzled it?

"Knowing about the gold and really where it now lay, I approached your uncle given his reputation in recovering treasure," began Andrew. "Your uncle was very interested and told me that he had been planning with Gregory to go to the cave and carry out a salvage operation. His research on the General Grant and its resting place was very good but flawed by the belief that the treasure was still in the cave. We quickly planned a covert salvage operation with both Gregory and your uncle insisting and stressing that we say nothing to anyone."

"Like the IRD," I commented.

"More than just IRD," replied Andrew, smirking. "You need permission from the Marine Department, then there's the Department of Conservation who administer the islands, and any items recovered could involve the Ministry for Culture and Heritage and even the Australian government. Gregory and your uncle were right as it just gets too messy and your share gets substantially reduced. It boils down to the story of the little red hen; nobody wants to do the work but everyone wants a piece of the booty. Many salvage operations have been done on the quiet and probably much of what we believe still lies on the seabed worldwide has quietly been salvaged."

"I'm no expert on boats, but I would've thought that questions would be asked when you docked in at a fishing port like Bluff Harbour," I said. "The fishermen there, I'd imagine, would be very protective of their territory and watchful for any intruder threatening their livelihood. Being such a small place, news would circulate quickly."

"And you're right," replied Andrew. "That's exactly why we left from Dunedin and travelled past Bluff and Stewart Island during the night otherwise we would have been spotted by a fishing boat. Once at the Auckland Islands we didn't have these problems as the place is so remote that nobody would be there to see us. We spent the next day with two people underwater and one on top."

"Did my uncle dive?"

"Ha, ha, now that's very funny. Your uncle - a diver?" laughed Andrew. "Putting on a diving suit and going down into the depths doesn't make you a diver, Robert. It's a different world down there with different rules and you need to understand the behaviour of the various fish. You often get little warning if a shark is on the prowl and you need to know how to handle such a situation. Your uncle, I'm afraid to say, was no diver. An adventure lover, yes, but he was never comfortable in an underwater environment he didn't fully understand. Suffice to say he was a worrier and needed to be in control."

"So that's where I get it from," I laughed.

"If you recall, at your uncle's funeral, I spoke about a treasure-hunting expedition off the Queensland coast of Australia. On this occasion, your uncle dived but very quickly returned to the surface when he spotted a Port Jackson shark swimming near the sea bed. There was no way we were going to get him back into the water that day."

"I don't blame him," I replied. "I'd be up and out of the water as soon as possible if I saw a shark."

"That's my point," said Andrew. "Port Jacksons and many other sharks are quite harmless and if you leave them alone then they'll reciprocate. We swim amongst sharks quite often; it's just you need to know which ones are harmless and recognise a threatening situation."

"When I approached your uncle he was more than happy with me being part of the expedition as he had heard of the Stewart Island area as being a popular gathering for the Great White Shark. These days you can pay to go down in a shark cage to view them. It's a popular tourist attraction."

"You wouldn't get me doing that." I shrugged my shoulders.

"If there are Great Whites around Stewart Island," continued Andrew, "then there are likely to be some further south like the Auckland Islands and these are the most dangerous of the shark family. Your uncle probably wouldn't see one coming, let alone know what to do. I'm not sure how they'd have got on had he and Gregory just gone. The weather can also change so quickly and, given the small window of opportunity, you need more than one diver to find and recover what you can while you can. First, we needed to find the treasure."

"It would be like looking for a needle in a haystack," I commented.

"So you're a farmer," laughed Andrew. "Not quite, as we were able to sweep the whole area with a magnetometer to detect any metal. As you can appreciate, the gold after a hundred years will be buried in amongst all the muck on the seafloor. In addition, visibility isn't that great underwater and once we start stirring up the muck on the bottom it becomes quite murky and even worse for visibility. In particular, we're also looking for shapes that look out of place like humps and bumps which might be the bags of spelter or one of the sunken boats. Now gold is quite different, even underwater it looks like gold. Once we had found one gold bar we were on to it and it didn't take long to find more. The bars all seemed to be in the one small area and would've fallen out together as the boats were together when they capsized. There were other shapes worth investigating but Gregory was insistent that we focus on the gold bars and any gold or silver coins we found. He said that we didn't have time to waste on investigating the spelter if it was there. As it was, the weather looked ominous and we knew it could change quite quickly. We didn't want to end up like earlier salvage attempts going away empty-handed. At the time it made a lot of sense and it was his boat at risk of capsizing if the seas suddenly became turbulent. Others had died in the search for the treasure, and other salvage operations had come to an abrupt end due to bad weather, so it was a pragmatic approach and what we recovered was worth millions."

"So you cleared out the gold and got out before you became another failed salvage operation?"

"Exactly, the weather conditions give you a small window of opportunity and we took it. I guess that greed can get the better of you and there's always just one more load to retrieve but fortunately we settled for what we could recover in that time. I have a lovely home to show for it," replied Andrew.

"So how did you manage to move and sell the gold?" I asked.

"Oh yes, a very good question, Robert. That was the tricky part and where Gregory with his connections came in as very useful. We sailed back by night to Dunedin and off-loaded your uncle's share of the gold bars into the back of a truck. Gregory and I then continued sailing to Auckland where we moved the gold to a warehouse and Gregory found buyers. It wasn't that difficult to sell as some of his wealthy friends wanted gold to hide their wealth. We didn't have to discount it at all."

"Hide their wealth, Andrew?"

"That's a good question," he replied. "If you have your money in a bank or shares then others can soon establish your net-worth and of course there's the IRD who can look into your bank records and investments to ensure that you're paying your fair share of tax. Now what you have in gold, precious stones and artwork is a different story. Gold is also useful for money laundering." Andrew rose to take the used coffee cups to the kitchen.

"Are you talking about criminals?"

"Crime, tax, whatever," replied Andrew. "Gold is of use for dodgy people like Gregory."

"And my uncle's gold?"

"I was hoping that you would know about this because I would like my share of the other gold. If the gold wasn't in his inheritance payout then he must have it stashed away with my share of the bagged gold. I doubt that he'd have spent it as he was already a wealthy man after finding the pirates' treasure," said Andrew. "Gregory only cashed in our gold."

"And that's the mystery," I replied, "as he only lived on the farm and never owned any properties nor even a car in New Zealand."

"Well, there you go, it must still be on your farm somewhere then. Maybe in a place like a barn," replied Andrew. "There again, people have been known to hide gold under their floorboards, or maybe he has it in storage somewhere. I'm sure he would have left you with a key, note or something leading to its whereabouts before he died."

"You might be right about the barn," I replied. "As well as winter feed it's full of obsolete rusty equipment and other rubbish and would be ideal for hiding something of value. I guess it's worth looking into and it's well overdue for a tidy up."

"So, how are you planning on getting back to your hotel?" Andrew asked, looking at his watch. It became clear that he wasn't offering lunch.

"I was going to catch a bus to town then another to Mangere," I replied.

"Look, I'll save you the bother and drop you there myself. I was going out anyway and it doesn't take long on the motorway." Andrew led the way to his late-model BMW parked in the drive and we set off.

Chapter 19

"Make your choice, adventurous stranger,

Strike the bell and bide the danger,

Or wonder till it drives you mad,

What would have followed if you had?"

C.S. Lewis

"Other Kiwis are scared of our Auckland motorway," commented Andrew, as he switched lanes. "But when you have to use it every day you think nothing of it. It's just that many New Zealanders aren't used to lane driving and of course, it does help if you know what lane you're supposed to be in. There's nothing worse than getting stuck in the wrong lane then finding you have to unintentionally leave the motorway and find a way back."

"I'll believe you," I replied, "and I'm quite happy with our single-lane highways and gravel country roads. I do like your BMW though, it's very smooth and comfortable. It's so quiet, unlike the tractor back home."

"Well, when you find the gold you'll be able to afford one too," laughed Andrew. "Though I really would like my share of the other gold otherwise I might have to downsize to a tractor."

"I might have to burn down the barn yet to find it," I joked. "The barn's old and the roof needs replacing anyhow. I could do with a new barn. Changing the subject, after the General Grant did you do any more diving with my uncle other than the reef off the Australian coast?"

"Yes, I did. Once you find a treasure like the General Grant then greed sets in and there's a craving for more and more wealth; for finding more treasure. One's hunger is never satisfied. The General Grant enabled our family to buy a fantastic house but unfortunately, I still needed to work to pay off the day-to-day bills. At the time I thought that if we could just find another General Grant then I could chuck in my job and live comfortably off investments. But life doesn't work like that, especially in finding sunken treasure ships which is very much a lottery. Numerous salvage operations fail, many through bad weather and in some cases like the General Grant, treasure-hunters lose their lives. In this case, we had the only winning lottery ticket due to insider information and even then it wasn't at all straight forward. Finding wrecks is no simple task because everything on the sea bottom looks the same and can get moved around like clothes in a washing machine. Even when you find a wreck there's no guarantee that you'll find treasure. Nearly everything apart from gold takes on a dull greyish look, even silver, so you have to dig around on the ocean floor." Andrew paused to toot at a vehicle that had crossed from the next lane cutting in front of him.

"Yes, I joined your uncle and Gregory on another diving trip off Australia and we found the wreck we were looking for, but the gold and silver coin haul was disappointing and hardly sufficient to meet our expenses. On these trips, your uncle was always very secretive and he would say "tell no one." It made sense as the Australians have these rules for what you can recover from wrecks. Gregory would add to this by saying, "Rules are meant to be broken," then laugh. In Auckland, he has a reputation for being an unscrupulous businessman and he employs expensive accountants and solicitors to cover his tracks. I wouldn't trust him as far as I could throw him. Anyhow, after that disappointing dive, I decided that treasure-hunting was a waste of time, more of a lottery but without the fun of being able to share any success."

"So you didn't do any more then?" I asked.

"OK, so it's hard to change." Andrew turned a slight pink colour. "The reality is that diving is in my blood and your uncle approached me with a hard to turn down proposition. Have you heard of the Flor de la Mar or Flower of the sea?"

"What on earth's that?" I replied.

"It was a Portuguese merchant vessel and it was involved in the capture of Malacca. Have you been there in your travels?"

"No, I'm just a rural lad and have little incentive to travel. The only place I've been to outside of New Zealand is Bali."

"Well, Malacca is strategic in controlling the Straits of Malacca and is part of Malaysia. It was conquered by the Portuguese who in turn were conquered by the Dutch who later sold it to the English, so it has quite a history. It's an amazing place with Arabic architecture, some remains of the Portuguese fort and a lot of orange Dutch buildings. Anyhow, I'm digressing so I'll get back to the story."

"In the sixteenth century, the Sultanate of Malacca was one of the richest cities in the world. In 1511 the Portuguese sent a number of ships including the Flor de la Mar to capture Malacca and were successful. The Flor de la Mar, being a three-mast transport vessel, was loaded up with most of the treasures of the Sultanate and sent on its way to Lisbon, but it sank during a violent storm off the coast of Sumatra in the Straits of Malacca. In fact, the ship was split apart and was not only carrying the treasure of the Sultanate but also an impressive tribute form the King of Siam to the King of Portugal. It's probably the richest ever treasure to be lying at the bottom of any ocean."

"Lots of gold?" I suggested.

"Probably, but lots of diamonds and other precious stones."

"So, did you find anything?"

"As your uncle says, 'tell no one'." Andrew laughed then hesitated. "The answer is no. It's not the easiest place to dive with its strong currents and murky waters and like many, many other treasure-hunters we came up empty-handed. It's still down there on the bottom of the ocean waiting for some lucky divers," Andrew said.

"So that treasure hunt was with my uncle and Gregory?" I asked.

"Well, fortunately, this time Gregory wasn't involved. The other diver was an Australian called Wally," Andrew said, as he left the motorway.

"Wally! Wally Devine, an Australian?" I said in disbelief.

"Yes, that's the name, why do you know him?" asked Andrew. "You seem rather surprised."

"Wally Devine? It's just so hard to believe after all I'd been told. Yes, I have met him. So when was this?"

"Oh, in the 1990s," replied Andrew.

"Wally Devine, really, that recent? So how did my uncle and Wally get on during the treasure hunt?" I was still somewhat stunned as this was well after my uncle and Martha had deserted Wally.

"They got on very well as good friends do and worked well together. I was the one who found Wally hard to communicate with. He's a hard man with whom I chose my words carefully lest I ended up with a fist in my face. I wouldn't want to get offside him. Why do you ask?"

"Ah, just he and my uncle had a bit of a problem over a woman," I replied.

Andrew laughed. "Oh, now that wouldn't be Martha would it?"

"Yes, have you met her?"

"Oh, goodness no, thank goodness, not after all the things they said about her. So, do you want me to drop you off at the hotel?" Andrew had now left the motorway and was driving through Mangere.

"The town centre will be fine. I need to purchase my lunch and other food supplies. Presumably, there will be a supermarket." I looked out the window and saw the town centre ahead.

"The town centre," said Andrew, bringing his BMW to a stop. "Your hotel is just down the road and turn right. I'd hide that watch as this is not the sort of place you'd flash a Rolex."

"Thank you," I replied, pulling down my sleeve.

"Keep in touch. I look forward to hearing from you when you find that booty," Andrew smiled. "Just remember that some of those bags of gold are mine and I'm depending on them for my retirement."

I wandered towards the town centre past the bus stop where I had taken the bus into town. Auckland was not at all like my quiet laid-back Gore. Here, even in the suburbs, the roads were busy and noisy. Inside Mangere town centre, it was no better, being somewhat crowded as if there was a sale on. It seemed like I was the only white face as I pressed past Asians and Pacific Islanders. I pulled my jersey sleeve down again to hide my Rolex and placed my right hand in my trouser pocket to secure my wallet as a sense of paranoia crept in, contributing to my anxiety and claustrophobia. I now viewed each passing face with distrust. It was the same feeling that I had had since the third day in Bali of being followed. Perhaps I was still under surveillance, but by who remained a mystery. This was a poor neighbourhood and I was a prime target for anyone criminally-minded. I now nervously continued through the covered arcade, past an Asian veggie market and fruit shops, towards the supermarket. So this is how it must feel for a coloured person in a European setting where everyone else is white. The supermarket was at the end of the arcade and, to me, this large western-style shop felt more familiar and like a sanctuary. I walked down the various wide aisles searching for food that might satiate my appetite. I had been in very few supermarkets in my life so the filing system was a mystery, though I have to say better than the system I used on the farm. At home what I needed was filed where I had last used it. I looked across the aisles which seemed relatively deserted. The large Samoan man in the second aisle seemed to be watching me or was that my imagination again? Perhaps it was because I looked lost. I moved to another aisle and shortly after he followed, which Mary would have described as being purely coincidence. Finally, I found what I was looking for, a packet of sandwiches, and left for the counter. I looked behind me and the big Samoan man was now also coming to the counter with a handful of items.

Before returning to my hotel I decided that I might as well explore the rest of the mall despite feeling uncomfortably conspicuous. Out the back of the mall was a market set up in the car park. It was selling all sorts of interesting items, many handmade reflecting island culture. Once again I was the only white face but I was curious to view what was on display. I wound my way through the stalls to those at the very back. My shirt suddenly felt taut around my neck. A firm arm had grabbed me from behind. I dropped my sandwiches as I struggled and was dragged backwards like a sheep to the shearing platform. I was being pulled out of sight behind a tent. Then in front of me stood a solidly built Pacific Islander who glared at me, before pulling my head up painfully by the hair.

"I want the gold," and with that, he punched me hard in the stomach and immediately I doubled over breathless. He pulled my head up again by the hair then smashed his large fist into my face. I could feel the blood now warmly running from my nose as the other man behind let me fall backwards hard to the ground where my head crunched on the hard asphalt. For a few minutes, my head was in a spin but I instinctively brought my hands over my head as protection. I could feel my body being kicked, but I lay helpless.

"You'll be hearing more from us," laughed the Islander, as he finally stopped kicking and removed my gold ring and Rolex watch. Then both men fled as the locals arrived quickly to my rescue. Others at the market had already called the police and an ambulance and in New Zealand, you can always be pretty confident that the ambulance will always win.

"No, don't move," advised one of the onlookers as I tried to find my legs. It was the large Samoan man. "You don't know what may have been broken. Wait for the paramedics."

My vision was a blur but I could now make out the ambulance people as they bent over me and prodded my body for broken bones before lifting me carefully onto a stretcher and into the ambulance. On the way to the hospital, one started to question me about whether I had blurred vision, whether I could move my toes and fingers and whether I had pain anywhere. Of course, I had pain everywhere, especially after having been kicked on the ground. Just the fall on the hard pavement had nearly cracked my skull or maybe it had. At the hospital, I was forced to ride in a wheelchair despite my protests as I was still more than capable of walking. It was undignified for a country lad who in his heyday thought nothing about hurdling the fences especially when there was a bull on his tail. I was signed in so as to speak then sent to an accident and emergency curtained cubicle where I was first interrogated by a nurse before a doctor finally rescued me, asking similar but more in-depth questions.

"No apparent fractures," said the doctor after checking my ribs and asking me if any area hurt when he applied pressure. He also carried out tests for concussion.

"Well, it looks like you've been pretty well knocked about but have survived miraculously," reported the doctor. "This type of situation can often end up quite ugly. If there are any sudden pains or other problems then come back to A and E. You're free to go."

"Not just yet," said a Maori policewoman who I hadn't noticed standing in the background. "I'm Sergeant Smith and it would be helpful if you can give me some details. Now, first, let me get a statement of what happened." She produced a notebook and pen and began writing.

I explained to her that I was just looking around the market when I was set upon.

"Did you get a good look at your attacker?"

"There were two. One I didn't see and the other was a well-built Islander. Maybe he was Samoan or Tongan. I live in the far south of the South Island and I don't see many Pacific Islanders, so I really can't tell the difference. Ah, but one thing, he had a small tattoo star under his left eye." I had now moved from a position of lying on the bed to one of sitting up where I could see the police officer more clearly.

"Now the tattoo is very helpful, almost as good as a fingerprint. I think I know who one of your assailants may be. Did they say anything when they attacked you or did you provoke them in any way?"

I paused as I didn't want to bring up the General Grant and make more people think that I may have the treasure.

"Well, he said he wanted the gold and would be in touch," I replied. "There was no provocation on my part."

"Gold?" Sergeant Smith looked puzzled. "Are you carrying gold?"

"Just my Rolex and a ring and they took them both," I replied.

"I will need details on the ring and Rolex," said the sergeant reopening her notebook. "And you don't know either of your assailants?"

"No, I don't know them and I've never lived in Auckland. This is a long-shot but my uncle was an explorer of sorts and was known to have found treasure. I inherited his fortune — that is what was left of it, and there's talk that there might be further treasure somewhere in the form of gold. Quite ridiculous as his estate has been finalised and there's no gold," I added.

"So you don't have any other gold then, Robert?"

"No, not that I am aware of. I live on a farm in Gore and I guess my uncle could have hidden it or buried it somewhere but I certainly don't have any gold. Colin, the local constable knows all about this and suggested that I tell no-one which has proven wise advice in hindsight."

"Colin? Why of course, he was on my team before moving down to Gore — for him probably a very good move being a rural man at heart and uncomfortable with the type of crime we have to face in South Auckland." The sergeant paused in thought for a few seconds then her face dropped and she mumbled, Ka mua, ka muri."

"Sorry, I don't understand what you're saying," I said.

"I was thinking aloud in Maori," replied the police sergeant as she regained her composure. "So you don't know the Maori language?" she asked.

"No," I replied.

"You should," said the sergeant. "Every New Zealander should. I know, there are not many Maori down your way and that your generation never got to learn Te Reo, but that's no excuse. We are one country; kotahi tatou."

"Sorry?"

"We become one", replied the sergeant. "I'm a descendant from the Ngai Tahu, a South Island iwi."

"Yet you live in Auckland?"

"Yes, of course, our tribal territory these days are no longer a constraint. What I said in Maori before is an old Maori proverb," replied the sergeant, "that translates as walking backwards into the future. In other words, we need to look back to the past as we move on towards the future."

"That's very profound," I replied.

"Yes, but worthwhile you thinking about, Robert. Now, what did you say they stole?"

"My signet ring and my Rolex watch. The watch has my uncle's name engraved on the back and the ring has a male lions face and is gold."

"Good, an engraved name will make things much easier for us," said the police sergeant. "So what are your plans now?"

"My plane leaves for Dunedin late tomorrow morning and I was about to return to my hotel in Mangere when I was assaulted. I'm not sure where I am now but I guess there will be a bus or taxi somewhere to get me back. I also need to find a supermarket or food outlet as I lost my lunch when I was assaulted."

"Not surprising," said the policewoman. "Vomiting after such an experience is to be expected."

"No, I mean I dropped the sandwiches I was carrying," I clarified.

"Oh, sorry. Look, Mangere is my beat, so I can drop you back at your hotel and we can stop somewhere on the way if you need to buy food. It would be good to have a chat on the way and find out how Colin's coping if you don't mind riding in the police car," the sergeant laughed. "I promise I won't handcuff you this time."

"Thank you," I replied. "Fortunately I still have my wallet so I think I'll buy something for tea as well as I now have an aversion to returning to Mangere Town Centre."

"I don't blame you," the sergeant replied. "I wouldn't wish this on anyone."

Chapter 20

"What do you tell a man with two black eyes? Nothing, he's already been told twice."

Elmore Leonard

"Whatever happened to you?" Mary asked as she noticed my somewhat rearranged face.

"Certainly a couple of shiners," Harry smirked. "Was it the diver or the bank manager?"

"And you were worried about Wally," laughed Mary. "It was probably the girl behind reception, Harry."

"No, I was assaulted at a market in Mangere, but I fear that it's related to my uncle's gold. They took my watch and signet ring, but I still have my wallet and credit card."

"Don't be so paranoid," Mary responded. "I thought you'd finally come to your senses and accepted that the General Grant never happened. Even the old feller in Bali implied as much. When you go to big cities like Auckland, you've got to remember that it's not Gore and you need to be careful where you wander. You just happened to be in the wrong place at the right time."

"A fairly crowded street market in the middle of the day, Mary? I don't think so. It would have to be one of the safest of places. And it was about the gold as one of the villains threatened me with more of the same if I didn't hand over the gold."

"Come on dear, get real. When they said gold they were talking about your watch and ring. It certainly stood out after it was cleaned up."

"Another shiner," laughed Harry. "They did a swap, that's what happened. Two for the price of one, haha."

"Or simply a mistake in identity because we don't have any gold," Mary added. "Just pure coincidence and you're so paranoid. Really, who's going to know that you're up in Auckland or that on the spur of the moment you decided to visit a street market?"

"Well, Mary, the diver confirmed that my uncle's salvage did take place on the wreck of the General Grant and he has a nice house to prove it," I replied. "Now he has no reason at all to lie. So I guess that I haven't been paranoid after all. Since we've been in Bali I could swear that at times I've been followed in both Gore and Auckland."

"Oh dear," sighed Mary. "Now we're back onto being followed again and the gold having been salvaged?"

"The fact is that, whether we like it or not, my uncle salvaged the General Grant treasure. The real question is where would he have put it?"

"Over half a century he would've probably have spent it then if that's the case," dismissed Mary. "He would have needed money to live on and to finance ventures. Finding old wrecks and sizeable treasures is not something treasure-hunters do every day or even every year. Why on earth would he hold onto it if they recovered it in the seventies? You really didn't know your uncle at all: the gun and passports and who knows what else? You know nothing about his lifestyle and what he did overseas. With all his wealth he could have quite easily gambled it away or lost it in the stock market crash. Yes, that's probably what happened."

"That's true," I sighed. "I thought I did know him but you may very well be right."

"Well, I for one would agree that you're not paranoid, Dad," said Harry, coming to my defence. "While you were away I saw drones with cameras flying all over our farm. Now, who would be doing this and why?"

"Drones over my farm?" I was shocked. "What the…that's an invasion of privacy. They can't do that. You should have shot them down, Harry. It would have been good practice with the shotgun."

"Not you too." Mary looked worried.

"What a cheek. Next time, Harry, you have my permission, just shoot them down. Maybe they were looking for the treasure," I replied. "Add to this the lifted floorboards, my being chased in Bali, assaulted in Auckland; I would say things are now looking a tad more than just coincidence Mary." I touched one of my eyes which still felt tender.

"That looks sore." Mary looked concerned. "Would you like me to bathe it?"

"I don't need a fuss," I replied. "I'll get over it."

"While you were out getting your face job we had a break-in," announced Harry, looking towards Mary who suddenly became quite upset.

"And your uncle's pearl necklace is gone," sobbed Mary. "Looks like it happened when I was out at a church women's meeting and Harry was out in a far paddock turning over the soil. That seems to be the only thing taken, sniff, though the little red notebook I religiously keep by my bed—the one I use for bible studies, has also disappeared. Colin came over and carried out a thorough search through the house looking for evidence."

"Did he find any?"

"No. Well let's admit it — your uncle didn't keep good company," said Harry. "That's for sure. Colin was telling me about the crooked lawyer and dodgy accountant and your uncle's shady partner."

"Then there's that creepy Jack who you never should have employed," said Mary, now more composed. "If we find the gold…" Mary chuckled. "And pigs might fly. Now you've got me going. I think that Colin is right and we'll need police protection."

"Tomorrow is going to be good weather to do the crutching and drenching," I said, looking at Harry, "and if that all goes to plan then maybe later in the week we can spring-clean the barn if you're free. If there's any gold in there then we'll surely find it. Other than burying it I can't see where uncle would hide gold bars. I'm inclined to agree with you, Mary, that it has somehow been all used despite my uncle having the pirates' treasure which would have been more than sufficient to live off."

"Fine with me. There's a lot of junk in there," Harry joked. "I suggested years ago that we needed to take all that rubbish to the metal merchant rather than leaving it to rust away. You'd have so much more room for your new tractor. There's even an old Morri somewhere buried in that lot, but given its state now no car collector would be interested."

That evening I caught up with Colin at Traffers. He had not been assigned to traffic duties so he was in a very good mood and was pleased to see me.

"Well, what do we have here, a couple of shiners? I never thought that Mary had it in her but she looks like she can pack a good punch. Never argue with a woman, Robbie."

"Not Mary," I replied. "I received these in Auckland after visiting the diver."

"He did that? Now don't tell me your uncle upset him as well?"

"No, the diver was most accommodating except he could have offered me lunch. He does want his share of the other gold though."

"Other gold?" Colin looked interested. "What do you mean by other gold?"

"The General Grant was also carrying something like 70 ton of spelter," I explained.

"Spelter?" Colin asked. "What on earth is spelter?"

"I understand it to be a light metal, I think mostly zinc. It was used to make figurines and other artwork. But it is not of high value and when ships at that time were few and far between and each voyage between Australia and England dangerous, it does raise the question as to whether the bags instead contained alluvial gold. Add the fact that most of the passengers were gold miners, with little trust in banks, who were returning to England after years of mining. Both the diver and I though the spelter could very well be their gold."

"So, let me get this straight, by using the words other gold, you're now admitting that your uncle found the gold bars from the General Grant? I knew you weren't being straight with me." Colin poured another glass of beer.

"Well, the diver claims to have found the gold and says that's how he could afford such a nice home, but everyone else I have spoken to, including my uncle's old partner, has essentially said the opposite and as I keep telling you I do not have the gold."

"Sure," Colin replied. "His old partner is still alive?"

"Fit as a fiddle," I replied.

"And living in New Zealand?"

"No, Colin not in New Zealand. As for my black eyes, these resulted when I was confronted by two unsavoury characters at a street market in Auckland."

"Not like you to pick a fight," commented Colin.

"And I didn't. These two big guys appeared from nowhere and suddenly started punching and kicking me. One says to me that he wants my gold."

"Ah! There you go and I told you so. I warned you." Colin glared at me. "You didn't listen and had to blab to everyone about the General Grant and now you've involved the criminal world and this is even in Auckland, Robbie."

"Mary thinks that the assailant meant my Rolex as they took that and my ring," I added.

"Hardly." Colin picked up his glass. "They'd have no reason when they could take them regardless. No, these people mean business and will stop at nothing till they get your uncle's gold. Believe me, you could be in for much more than a black eye."

"Oh, I forgot to mention that Harry had seen a drone checking out our property."

"Ah, further evidence. So, there you go," replied Colin. "The floorboards, assault, theft and now the drone. They'll stop at nothing but I did warn you."

"I guess you're right," I replied. "And it's hard to know who might be behind this as my uncle mixed with some unscrupulous characters."

"I was also followed in Bali," I added. "But the guys who assaulted me weren't the same people."

"They don't need to be," replied Colin. "Some of these criminals have overseas contacts. You need to be more trusting of your local police force so we can ensure that your gold is safe and we can catch whoever is behind this. I suspect Jack and that pastor guy who have both made many contacts while in prison."

"There's no gold as I keep telling you, Colin, and I've spent enough time investigating this," I replied. My farm work is falling behind and I need to spend the week catching up as there's a lot to do."

Chapter 21

"My sheep listen to my voice;

I know them and they follow me."

John 10:27

Crutching and drenching the sheep is such a big job as we first also need to muster the flock which can be a timely process. Often in mustering, you can almost guarantee that there will be a breakaway group of sheep who choose their moment then double back and break the line. Their body language, especially the look in their eyes, is often a giveaway. This is where the dogs with their speed come in handy. A bit of barking, and occasionally a sharp nip on the bum, eventually brings the offenders back into line.

Harry wasn't overly keen on our rushed programme but he was also concerned that lambing had already started and too much time had been wasted on my uncle's affairs. These new lambs needed tail docking, vaccinating, drenching, shearing and for the males, castration. The adult sheep in particular needed crutching as the wool around their bottoms can otherwise get quite messy. Attending to the sheep had now become a high priority. Of prime concern to Harry was that the sheep wouldn't have emptied as we were taking them straight from the pasture through the holding pens to the shearing platform. Sheep, when they haven't emptied, are high spirited and more difficult to handle on the shearing floor. Normally the sheep would be left in the holding pens where there was no food for an hour or two at least which I did not have.

Harry grabbed the motorbike and the two dogs and I took off after him in the tractor and we headed towards one of the larger paddocks where we had many ewes and new-born lambs. While Harry and the dogs got in behind the sheep I came from one side steering the flock towards the open gate. The sheep eventually got the message and filed through the open gate and up onto the drive. One of the stragglers was a mother with twins who was showing life-threatening evidence of fly-strike. With the other 'dirty sheep' she would be fully shorn and treated with cyromazine to kill the maggots.

Once we had squeezed all the sheep into the holding pens and forced the gate closed we separated them: the dirty sheep went in one pen, the lambs into another and the rest, making up the majority, remained in the larger area. First, we attended to the lambs, Harry and I finally shearing them before sending each back down a chute to the holding pens and their mothers. Mary had joined us and was bunching up the wool clippings and throwing them into a bale reserved for this finer wool. After the lambs, we attended to the dirty sheep by shearing them in total so we could see the full extent of maggot infestation and treat it. This wool was kept separate. We hoped to complete the rest of the sheep by lunchtime, each sheep taking about a minute to crutch.

Harry and I had completed all but twenty ewes when I heard a voice above the electric shears.

"I couldn't find anyone at the house so I followed the loud baaing sound." It was the pastor and true to form he had arrived just before lunch. He was quite pleased with himself, having used his investigative skills successfully.

"Thank you for coming," replied Mary. "It's one of our big days as you can see."

"Can I help?" offered the pastor.

"All the discoloured wool from the crutching goes into this bag but don't go near that one." Mary pointed to the bale holding lamb wool.

"OK," said the pastor as he picked up two handfuls of wool.

"I heard about your husband being beaten up and came to see if he's alright?" the pastor continued. "It must be a difficult time for him."

"He's managing," replied Mary, "but yes he's still sore all over and I imagine after all this hard work today he'll be soaking in a hot bath."

"On a farm, life has to continue no matter what," I yelled above the shearing noise. "There's no rest for the wicked."

The pastor and Mary laughed. I probably didn't look a pretty sight in a moth-eaten singlet with my black eyes, greasy hair and sweat dripping off my forehead.

"Very physical work," commented the pastor as I returned to the shearing floor dragging a large ewe. "Robbie is very strong."

"There's a lot in technique; shearing is a skill learned over many years," added Mary.

"Even the wool clearing is hard work," the pastor paused puffing. "This wool just keeps coming. One can certainly build up a craving for food working at this pace."

"You're welcome to stay for lunch," replied Mary smiling, "but because this is a very busy day we'll only be grabbing a quick snack then I'm afraid it's back to mustering another paddock of ewes and lambs, drenching crutching and everything else. When we get started it's full-on all day."

"Maybe I could help with the mustering after lunch," replied the pastor, who had imagined that a snack in a farmer's wife's language meant much more than just a vegemite sandwich and would be worth staying for.

"I'm sure Robbie would enjoy you tagging along," replied Mary smirking, "and not too difficult a job; they're just dumb old sheep," she lied.

Lunch turned out to be exactly that, a snack. Mary had been busy helping in the shearing shed so it was simply a help yourself to bread, butter and slices of meat or jam, whatever took your fancy. Mary put the boiled jug on the table with milk, tea bags and coffee and left it for each person to make their drink. It was certainly not the hospitality that the pastor had expected but his visit was, after all, to console me after my trauma in Auckland.

"So how are you feeling?" the pastor asked me with some concern, as I certainly didn't look the picture of health after crutching over a hundred sheep.

"Well, pretty exhausted after that last ewe who was kicking out and just wouldn't stay still. I was lucky not to knick her in the belly with the shears," I replied.

"No, I mean after Auckland, being mugged," clarified the pastor.

"Pretty rough," I replied. "Initially my vision was a bit blurred and my body ached all over."

"Have they caught them?" The pastor helped himself to his third sandwich and packed it generously with meat, tomato and lettuce.

"I haven't heard anything yet but they made off with my watch and ring." I took a bite of my mutton sandwich.

"A terrible thing," said the pastor. "To think I was once one of those nasty people. It's all about power and taking out one's frustrations on a world that has treated you so unfairly. When you're bullied by your parents as a child you're inclined to want to do the same to others. At the time you have no thoughts about the victim and what permanent damage you may be causing."

"I don't think this one was about power," I replied. "It seemed to me to be about the gold."

"Gold, Robbie? They were talking about your watch and ring." Mary frowned before looking over at the pastor to convey her concern.

"Robbie, Robbie, you need to put this gold thing behind you," the pastor said. "You didn't find any gold did you?"

"No," I replied, "but I won't know for sure until we clean out the barn."

"And when do you intend doing this?" the pastor helped himself to his fifth sandwich.

"A lot depends on how quickly we get the crutching done but I had planned on doing it this week."

"Tomorrow," said Harry, "or another year will pass and it will never be done."

"You need to get this gold business off your chest, Robbie, before it destroys you," said the pastor. "Best doing it tomorrow."

"Well, we better start moving to round up more sheep. It's all right we can drive to the paddock," I added as the pastor looked concerned at the thought of walking miles especially now that his stomach was satisfied and fully employed.

"And it's not too difficult?" asked the pastor who was starting to have second thoughts.

"Na, a piece of cake. All you have to do is stand there and pull faces at the sheep," laughed Harry.

Once we reached the paddock, Harry and I with the dogs carried out the same approach. He brought the sheep down from the top and I came in from the side. I asked the pastor to stand half a dozen metres from the open gate so the sheep would go up the drive rather than down.

"Just stand here," I said, "and wave your arms so the sheep don't try to pass you."

The pastor nervously waited as the sheep filed through the gate. Some continued up the drive while a rebellious group remained just past the gate giving the pastor the evil eye. Their intention was clear as the pastor soon found out, leaving him spinning in his tracks as they bolted and flew past on both sides. Still, only a half dozen managed to dodge the big man and the dogs soon sorted out the culprits.

"I think I would rather remain as a shepherd of people than sheep," commented a breathless pastor. "Though it does add meaning to the fact that we are all like sheep and have gone astray."

Chapter 22

"It's time for a spring cleaning of your thoughts, it's time to stop to just existing, it's time to start living."

Steve Maraboli

The next morning Harry and I decided to do a spring clean of the barn. If there were any gold bars on the farm then they had to be here. It was a bigger job than I'd envisaged because not only had I hoarded bits and pieces that I thought might be useful, but there was my father's and grandfather's junk as well. A lot of this clutter had accumulated after changing from a mixed farm to specialising in sheep. In New Zealand farming had changed over the last decades from being a blend of mixed farming to specialising in either mostly sheep or cows. As a result, we had old roofing iron that was once part of a piggery and other obsolete equipment from having had a small dairy herd. I looked at the old iron roofing stacked up in the barn and wondered where it could be used as it would be a shame to just throw this away. Perhaps it could be put aside as an addition to the hen house; maybe get a rooster and produce replacements for our ageing hens.

"Throw it out, Dad," Harry instructed as he saw me hesitate.

Together and reluctantly, in my case, we loaded each sheet onto the ute. It was a shame as the roofing looked to have life left in it. Then there was old worn-out machinery, broken equipment like a plough, bent and twisted fencing and lots of now useless toys and fun things from the past. There were times when some of these bits and pieces came in handy to solve a problem. For instance, a bit of old wire now and again was useful as a temporary binding measure, and it wouldn't have been the first time that an old tube had been modified saving the cost of a motor part. Each time that I hesitated, Harry was at my back.

"Throw it out, Dad."

I guess that he didn't want to inherit a farm full of rubbish accumulated over generations, but there was a lot of useful stuff here and some might become valuable as antiques. We loaded the obsolete machinery and other metal onto the ute and once it was loaded to capacity, Harry was quick, before I changed my mind, to set off to the metal merchant. I told Harry he could keep the proceeds which in the end didn't amount to much, despite numerous truck loads. I have to admit that it was nice to now see all four sides of the barn leaving a large enough area for the new tractor.

More importantly, we were now able to search from almost one end of the barn to the other but still there appeared to be no evidence of a stash of gold. Maybe we were missing something obvious like gold bars being painted over as bricks or lying in one of the many sacks we still needed to work through. Perhaps they were disguised in other ways amongst the remaining rubbish scattered throughout the barn or hidden behind the hay bales. I have to admit that it could have been staring me in the face and I probably wouldn't have seen it. As my mother used to tell me, I would have trouble even finding beer in a brewery.

"Enough of this nonsense," I said, as we both looked in the barn. While I was pleased with our accomplishment, I was somewhat frustrated by once again coming up empty-handed. "Harry, we still have more important things to do like shearing the remaining sheep and vaccinating and castrating the calves, and the fencing on that far paddock. Just a pity Jack left when he did."

"Agreed," replied Harry. "Jack, despite his appearance and body odour, was a lot of help. I also want to sow new grass in the paddocks I dug up the other day. Our lambs need to reach a good size for the freezing works."

Now that I had stopped working I put on my jersey as it was a chilly day. Mary came to join us at the barn so I gave her the bad news.

"And I could have told you that," reminded Mary, "but it's nice to see all that rubbish gone. As I've been trying to get through to you over and over again there is no gold. If your uncle had it then he would've cashed it in. There was no point him burying it somewhere on the farm that's for sure."

"Mary, you should tell Colin then, as he's convinced that we have the gold and is concerned for our safety. The two of you could have a fine old argument," I said.

"Robbie, just be grateful for the inheritance you've received. How many other farmers around here can brag about having a new tractor and new ute? I know that I'm looking forward to my new kitchen. Oh, I almost forgot to mention that your uncle's solicitor rang to say that he's about twenty minutes away and wanted to drop in a key that belonged to your uncle. He thought that it must have become separated from his other stuff. He was most apologetic."

"Another key? How many more of my uncle's keys does the man have?"

"Aha, finally the key to where the gold is being stored," Harry suggested, with a smirk on his face.

"Stop it, Harry." Mary frowned. "You mustn't wind your father up."

"Well, it might be the key to another safety deposit box and the gold," I said as we returned to the house to await his arrival.

"Don't get me started." Mary glared at Harry, just in case he was thinking of adding a further smart comment.

The solicitor arrived not long after in a late model Audi and was immediately made welcome by our two dogs.

"Same old farm," said the solicitor, looking at the house, up and down the drive and across the paddocks. "Not much has changed at all. You uncle's house is over there," he pointed. "And as I remember there was a big pond and a barn that way."

"You've been here before, then?" I looked surprised.

"Yes, of course, though many years ago. I remember the farm well from when I came to sort out your Aunt Betty's legacy with your dad."

"That's right," I replied, "but in those days you looked quite different; you were much younger."

"Of course he was, dear. Come in and have a coffee," offered Mary.

We all sat down at the table and Mary returned with drinks.

The solicitor produced an envelope. "Sorry, it's only a key to your uncle's post-box in Invercargill," said the solicitor, handing me the key, "but you never know what you may find."

"Of course." I took a sip, somewhat disappointed. "In hindsight, he had to have had a post-box as he never received mail on the farm. That would explain everything."

The solicitor looked at me with enquiring eyes. "How did you get on with your uncle's safety deposit box in Auckland?"

"You don't want to know," I replied. "I don't know how I am going to dispose of what's in there but let me say it's not lawful."

"No, no, don't tell me anything more. I don't want to know," replied the solicitor. "Your uncle was an enigma and always extremely secretive and I'm not surprised. And Wally, did you get to see him?"

"Seriously, how can anyone be terrified of an eighty-year-old man?" laughed Mary.

"Well, he's strongly built, fit and quite intimidating," I replied.

"So he didn't kill you then?" joked the solicitor. "And the gold, are you any wiser?"

"That was interesting," I replied. "My uncle, Martha and Wally had considered a salvage expedition to the Auckland Islands, but had decided that the treasure would have long gone."

"As I keep telling Robbie, there's no gold," Mary said. "They've even cleared out the barn now and the floorboards in Robbie's uncle's house have been lifted but there's no gold."

"The barn's not quite cleared out yet," corrected Harry, "but we're working on it aren't we, Dad? But I think that we'd have to burn down the barn to be absolutely sure there's no gold."

"What brings you down from Dunedin?" I asked. "Surely you didn't come all this way to deliver a key?"

"Oh, I have other business." The solicitor went a shade of pink. "You know I have been thinking about your comments and I agree that the inheritance does appear to be on the light side given the pirates' treasure and especially if your uncle did recover the gold from the General Grant. I don't trust your uncle's accountant at all. What did he say about the gold?"

"Didn't know anything about it, but he wouldn't put it past my uncle's partner Gregory to have got his hands on it."

"Has the accountant since enquired about the gold?" asked the solicitor.

"Well, come to think about it, he's the only one who hasn't," I replied.

"Interesting," the solicitor said. "The only one who hasn't. Why?"

"But we're now pretty sure that the gold never existed," Mary replied before I could say otherwise. She glared in my direction just in case I did.

"Oh well, who knows what this post-box might produce," said the solicitor. "Maybe even another key or instructions. Just remember that if you do find any more inheritance then legally it first needs to go through me as the executor of the will."

"Why's that?" asked Mary.

"Well, it's all part of the estate. Things must be done properly as set out under the law and you don't want the IRD knocking on your door sometime in the future." The solicitor placed his empty cup back on the saucer.

"Would you like a quick tour of the farm?" I offered.

"Thanks, but farm animals are not my thing," replied the solicitor, "and I have a long journey back to Dunedin ahead of me."

Chapter 23

"Whenever I'm asked what kind of writing is the most lucrative, I have to say ransom notes."
H.N. Swanson

The next morning I woke to the most delicious smell of bacon wafting through the house. I quickly rose, dressed and went to the kitchen where I found Harry devouring a plate heaped with rashers of bacon, fried eggs and hash browns.

"Morning Dad. Left you a few pieces of bacon that Mum's frying up now." Harry managed to say through a mouthful of breakfast.

"You deserve it, Robbie." Mary jumped back as a piece of fat exploded. "I've been rather hard on you lately, especially after losing your uncle and I hadn't realised that you were so close."

I sat down and Mary served me a delightfully large plate of bacon and eggs.

"Harry has agreed to take out our rubbish bins after breakfast," added Mary.

"I have?" replied a surprised Harry, smacking his lips, but ever so grateful after a delicious breakfast.

"And after that, we can round up what's left of the new lambs and maybe make a start on the shearing," I said.

Harry finished his meal and left the house to take the bins to the gate while I sat back and enjoyed what was left on my plate. Shortly afterwards the door flung open and in bounded Harry, somewhat distraught. "This note was pinned on our mailbox."

I unfolded the note which was marked urgent and read the contents. It started with "Let Auckland be a warning. Supply $2million in gold bars or cash as follows:" There were a lot of instructions such as loading the gold onto my new ute and leaving it and the keys at a certain remote place and time. It ended by saying, "Contact the police or fail to meet this request and you will meet with dire consequences."

My face dropped and initially, I hesitated before showing it to Mary.

"Well, it looks authentic and like they mean business," she said. "But of course this could just be a hoax from one of your farmer friends. The fact is we don't have any gold. I think you will need to show this to Colin."

"Exactly my thoughts." My body was still recovering from the last mugging and I was not ready for a repeat session. "I'll go into town straight away." I left the house and sped off in the ute, with both Mary and Harry watching, quite concerned about what might lie ahead. This matter was now getting totally out of hand.

"Colin's not here," said the duty sergeant. "Is there anything that I can help you with?"

"No, I should be OK," I lied. I thought it best to run the note through Colin first as it had said no police.

The duty sergeant looked at me. "Oh, before you leave, a police sergeant from Auckland rang just before you arrived. A sergeant…"

"Smith," I added.

"Yes, that's the name. She was, ah, wanting to catch up with you and is coming to Gore," continued the duty sergeant. "Has a tangi to attend in Invercargill and thought it a good time regarding the Auckland matter."

"Tangi?" I asked

"Yes, a Maori funeral. I think she lost a cousin," replied the sergeant. "Ah, Sergeant Smith asked that you keep her visit to yourself as she wanted to surprise Colin. I hear that she's a bit of a character and I'm looking forward to meeting her myself. Would you like me to tell Colin you dropped by?"

"Yes, please. Could you tell him that it's urgent and I'll catch up with him after work over a beer or two?"

"He'll appreciate that," replied the duty sergeant. "He's never happy when he's assigned to traffic duties and I'll warn you now that he'll be in a foul mood, but after a few beers he should come right."

"So I gathered," I replied.

That evening at Traffers I met with Colin.

"Yes, in hindsight you were right about keeping quiet about the gold and I think it'll get worse," I said, nervously pushing the note across the table.

"Who knows about this?" Colin looked concerned. "This is not at all looking pretty."

"I thought I'd check it out with you first rather than hand it to your duty sergeant."

"Good, very wise because one wrong move and somebody could get hurt. We want as few people involved as possible. Where's the gold now?"

"Colin, as I told you before, while my uncle may have salvaged the gold, I don't have it."

"Ah, at least that's a change from your position where you doubted the General Grant salvage operation ever took place. So now you finally admit the gold was salvaged, but for some reason, you still won't trust me. If you don't have it then you better find it very quickly as these people mean business. You haven't changed, Robbie. Even as a boy you'd only give me half the story."

"One thing which may be important, the note was on our letterbox and not our back door, which to me suggests that the person has been to our house before and knows about the dogs being housed by the door."

"That wouldn't surprise me at all," said Colin. "By now they would well and truly have checked out your property. I'm thinking that Jack and the pastor are in on this together with some friends in Auckland. What we need to do is to go along with the directions on the note and I can arrange to bring in a couple of my colleagues to spring a trap."

"That sounds to be a good plan Colin, if I had the gold," I replied.

Back in the house, Mary was quite worried about not meeting our deadline for paying the gold. She was well aware that we were being threatened by some nasty people. "No gold in the barn then?"

"No, and none on this farm," I replied.

"Then we need to get the police and not just Colin involved." Mary looked worried.

"You're right," I agreed. "They did say no police but we're sitting ducks out here in the country." I hesitated for a second. "I know what we can do, I'll call Sergeant Smith and run it past her after all this follows on from the assault. She did leave me her number and said to call if there were any problems or I remembered anything more about the assault."

Sergeant Smith was most happy to hear from me and had seemingly taken a shine to me, though I don't think it had anything to do with my black eyes. I explained what had transpired since Auckland.

She laughed. "I don't think you have too much to worry about if you don't meet their demands. We have now apprehended the two men who assaulted you. One was wearing your Rolex watch and the other we nailed after a suspicious metal merchant checked the ring out with us. We may need you to identify your assailants if they plead not guilty, but they were caught in possession and every indication is that they will confess. I will return your watch and ring when I'm in Gore later this week. Now please don't say anything to Colin at this stage."

"But these men will probably have accomplices in Gore," I replied, "otherwise how were they to collect the gold, which of course doesn't exist?"

"How indeed?" asked the sergeant. "I think with the two arrested and ready to sing, that you have nothing to worry about and we'll get to the bottom of it."

"Additional to the floorboards of my uncle's cottage being torn up and several days ago a drone hovering over our property, my wife had an expensive necklace stolen from the house. Are you able to look into that?"

"No, that should be handled by the local police. I can't just muscle my way into another district and police officer's case. That wouldn't go down well, a big city branch meddling in a small town police operation. It may not even be related, though I have to admit that it's certainly suspicious with all of these events happening within a short period. I'll catch up with you in a few days regarding the assault case."

"Good to know, goodbye," I replied, a much happier man as I ended our phone call.

"Nothing to worry about as they caught the two men who assaulted me," I told Mary. "But it's frustrating that we can't find any stash of gold."

"There's no gold," replied Mary. "Let it go."

Later in the day I caught up with Colin and told him that we were going to ignore the demand for gold.

"Mary said that it will be one of our farmer friends playing a joke."

"You're crazy and will be sorry," Colin replied. "You're dealing with hardened criminals who'll stop at nothing until you deliver. Somebody could get hurt and our branch operates on a shoe-string budget and isn't in any position, manpower-wise, to offer personal protection."

"They have already tried violence," I replied, pointing to my black eyes. "I agree, but there's no gold to deliver. We searched the barn and cleaned it out and other than burning it down to be absolutely sure, it does not look to be there."

"It's got to be," replied Colin. "If it's not in your uncle's house then maybe under the floorboards in your house, or failing that the shearing shed or hen-house."

"Ha ha, the shearing shed and the henhouse. Now that's very funny. Not much to see in those places. And our house, well my parents were living there and would have known. Dad would never have agreed to it. I don't know what happened to the gold but all I know is that it is not on the farm. My uncle must have sold it which would make sense, though he was already very wealthy. Why would he want to keep it all these years? Perhaps the solicitor or accountant haven't been totally honest and there's other money."

Colin frowned. "I'm sure it's there Robbie. In your own words, when your uncle was in New Zealand he only lived on the farm and owned no property. I doubt that the solicitor and accountant would put their careers on the line and risk the possibility of prison. Now we need a fool-proof plan to catch these crooks and this time don't tell anyone. It would be best to leave the gold as they have instructed but I can arrange with another couple of constables to lie in ambush. I think that this is the only way we're going to end this for good." Colin poured another beer. "What do you think?"

"Yes, it sounds a good plan…just that I don't have the gold," I said, looking quite agitated.

"I give up." Colin emptied his glass in one gulp and angrily rose from the table. "Do you want to put an end to this or not? If so then you'd better come up with it quickly because these criminals mean business."

Chapter 24

"There's some sort of magic in the unexpected."

Anonymous

Sergeant Smith was right as nothing happened the following days after failing to deliver on the extortionists' demands. Mary was now more relaxed and happy with Harry promising to stay around the house so I could make a trip to Invercargill. As it turned out the post-box was jam-packed, which was what one might expect given the fact that my uncle was incapacitated following his stroke and probably only emptied it between overseas adventures.

That night Mary and I sat on the floor and sorted through the mail. Reading through my uncle's private mail was an unnerving experience but gave us a larger window into his life.

"Looks like most of these letters have been opened already," Mary commented, as some of the parts on the envelope were no longer sticking.

"Well, only the solicitor had the key," I replied. "Are you suggesting that he was down in Invercargill reading through all the letters?"

"You're getting paranoid again," replied Mary.

"Hello, a letter from Martha." I pushed the letter in front of Mary. "See, the General Grant gold must exist as Martha is demanding her share in this letter."

"May exist," replied Mary. "But what is clear is that she may have been the one to stir up the tax department as she is threatening to go to the IRD if she doesn't get her share."

"And yet more letters from Martha," I said, pushing them all over to Mary.

"Hello, this looks to be a foreign bank account with substantial amounts invested," I said, as I separated the statements to find the latest balance.

"Now I'm not being paranoid, but do you think that the accountant may have made off with this money?" asked Mary pointing to a rather large balance.

"No," I replied producing a later statement. "The latest statement after his death shows a balance of $105,000 American. I think that the accountant may not have known about this. I will scan him a copy and get him to sort it out."

"I would copy in both your uncle's solicitor and our solicitor as well," suggested Mary, "just in case the accountant has other plans for the money. Make it clear to him that they're in the loop."

"Good thinking," I replied. "Well it looks like we've now accounted for the pirate's treasure," I added.

"Yes, I'd say so. You know these cruises your uncle went on sound very interesting." Mary held up a cruise brochure that was amongst the mail. "With this extra money, we could go on some of these cruises."

I frowned at the thought of being cooped up on a boat for several weeks on end without seeing much else but sea.

"It's not as bad as you think," Mary said, picking up on my body language. "Every day they provide buffets and this is included in the price, see?" Mary showed me the brochure.

With a buffet every day just maybe I could get to like cruise ships, I thought, but there would be no stopping Mary hitting the shops each time the ship reached port.

"I'm not so sure." I gave the brochures intentionally only a cursory glance before passing them back.

There was nothing much else in my uncle's mail apart from the results of a medical check-up which showed high blood pressure. Most of the items were junk mail like charities asking for donations and several cruise companies offering early-bird deals. One letter was from a friend inviting him on a cruise around South America which I'm sure he'd have taken had he not had the stroke at that time.

"Well, that was worthwhile finding out about Martha and the bank account," I summed up. Mary nodded her head in agreement.

With all my uncle's affairs now pretty much behind us we were able to continue farming and completing our work with the cattle. I still had that meeting in Gore with Sergeant Smith pending and was looking forward to getting back my watch and ring, both items I had become fondly attached to. There might also be news on Mary's necklace. Given the ransom note, these days, I didn't like leaving Mary on the farm at any time but Harry was going to be around, out in the paddocks sowing new grass seed and checking that the new-born lambs hadn't been abandoned by their mothers. With Romney ewes, twins are quite common but unfortunately, not all mothers want two lambs and sometimes they will reject one. In this case these lambs need to be hand-fed or they will die.

The day soon came around when I was to meet up with the sergeant. I set off in my new ute to Gore. Sergeant Smith was pleased to see me.

"Kia ora, you are looking much better than the last time I saw you." She gave me a big hug.

"Hello," I replied, smirking.

The sergeant led me into a room with several seats.

"This is certainly a change from the accountants' and solicitors' offices where they sat behind a desk," I said.

"Yes, many of these professionals are not that great with their communication techniques," replied the sergeant. "A desk in-between is certainly a barrier to open and frank discussion. So anyhow, here's your ring and watch." The sergeant handed me these items, plus a book. "Oh, this book is also for you to help you learn the Maori language."

"Thank you," I replied, placing the book down on the nearby table and returning the ring and watch to their rightful places.

So have you had any problems since failing to deliver the gold?" inquired the sergeant.

"No, you were right. I think that you must have done the damage when you arrested those two villains," I laughed.

"They should have been put away several months ago. One of Colin's cases but there was difficulty due to the chain of evidence," said the sergeant.

"Chain of evidence?"

"Yes, Robert. When you have evidence it must be documented, locked away and a record kept of when, who and where if it is removed. To give you an example, when Princess Diana was killed they took a blood sample of the chauffeur and it was reported that he had a high blood alcohol level. However, the blood sample taken before testing was left on a shelf overnight where anyone could have tampered with it. Because the chain of evidence was broken from when they removed it from his body to when they tested it, this is no longer evidence." The sergeant paused and looked quite puzzled. "What on earth is that noise?"

She sprung up and rushed to the window. "It sounds like an air raid siren and it can't be a tsunami, not this far inland."

"That's our voluntary fire brigade," I laughed. "Quite amusing to watch. The siren goes off then in the next five minutes or so volunteers: the butcher, baker and candlestick maker all turn up at the fire station on bicycles, motorbikes and cars. A few minutes later, the big red glass doors open and the fire engines burst out."

"Quite intriguing. In Auckland we have paid firemen," the sergeant smiled. "Colin isn't around today, on traffic duties I'm told. A pity as I was looking forward to surprising him."

"Yes, he loves his traffic duties…I think not," I replied, with a cheeky smile on my face.

The duty sergeant entered the room. "Just had a call from Harry, your son. He's out in the paddock and said the barn is on fire. Harry said not to worry as he was using your new tractor at the time and it is out in the paddock. Oh, he said Colin saw the fire and is at the scene."

"Another coincidence?" asked Sergeant Smith, "or do barns catch fire frequently and in winter?"

"It has to be arson," I replied. "There's no electricity to the barn to cause a fire. Sometimes if hay is wet and the outside temperature is hot there can be combustion, but in this case, I would suspect arson. Sorry, I'll catch you later, I need to go." I left the room quickly, giving me the excuse I needed to forget the book on the table.

Back at the farm, it was all activity with the firemen using our lake as a water supply. My grandfather would have been so pleased since he had created the lake for an emergency, even if he had been thinking more of a drought situation.

Colin was standing there right up at the frontline observing as the fire crew went about their task. They probably didn't see many fires in a small town, so this was good practice for something more serious like a house fire.

"You were lucky, the new tractor wasn't in there," shouted Colin over the background noise of hoses and crackling.

"Yes, I replied and lucky the barn was insured. I had planned on re-roofing it with some of my uncle's money."

"You didn't light it I hope?" Colin asked, smirking.

"No, of course not. I was in town at the time and wouldn't do such a thing, but I'd say it would have taken off very quickly with what remained of the winter feed."

"The hay bales, Robbie?"

"Yes, they'll add a lot of heat."

"Stand back — the metal roof is about to collapse." A fireman pushed us back.

There was an even louder creak and the main beam gave way with the whole roof structure crashing to the ground.

"It's a pity to see this old family barn finally end up like this," I sighed. "It must have been a hundred years old."

"At least you still have your farm. Everything comes to an end sometime," Colin replied. "Well I must be off or I'll get into trouble for not being out there giving speeding tickets. We must keep the government happy and bring in the money."

We watched for a little bit longer as the walls fell in then I turned to Harry who was somewhat fascinated by the whole firefighting operation.

"I think that we can leave the firemen to wet down the smouldering areas, Harry," I said. "Let's go and join your mum in the house. After this ordeal a cup of coffee would go down nicely."

Harry agreed and we walked back along the drive to the house. I was surprised that Mary hadn't come to observe the fire but with a recent break-in and strangers on our property somebody needed to be guarding the house.

"Mum's not here!" yelled a distressed Harry, who had decided in the end to run on ahead with the dogs, "but this ransom note was on the table. They never went away and now they have Mum."

"Let's see." I snatched the note out of Harry's hand. "So they want the gold in exchange for her. That's ridiculous. This has just gone too far."

I grabbed the telephone and called Sergeant Smith just as she was about to leave the Gore police station.

"OK! Calm down, there's absolutely nothing to worry about, Robert. There was more to my trip than just returning your watch and ring and attending a tangi. You'll have Mary back to you in no time, trust me."

As I put down the receiver the front door sprung open and three men carrying guns burst in. One I recognised as Wally Devine, and this time he looked more threatening than ever.

"You're both coming with us," Wally ordered. We were led out to a van and pushed into the back seats. On each side of us sat an armed man with a stone-cold face.

"I've looked everywhere but seriously, I don't have any gold," I replied. "Harry will confirm this. I don't even know if my uncle carried out the salvage of the General Grant."

"There's no gold, as my dad said. I just want my mum back," said Harry.

"You'll see her in good time. We're going for a drive." Wally looked like he'd stand no nonsense and now knowing what I did about him, we had no choice but to obey.

Chapter 25

"Emotions are captive to reality."

Kao Kalia Yang

The day of the fire Mary had been pottering around her kitchen deciding on what changes she wanted for her new kitchen. Finally, they were getting around to replacing their seventy-year-old kitchen. It was well and truly due for an overhaul with tight wooden drawers and badly aligned cupboard doors. She also rather fancied the thought of a wall oven; maybe a double oven that would enable her to cook a roast and dessert at the same time. She stopped to reflect on the past months that had been difficult for not only Robbie but the family. Grief over his uncle's death needed time to heal but she didn't like the negative effect it was having on him. He had become a different person: unsettled, moody, paranoid and in particular, obsessed with the General Grant.

"What am I going to do with Robbie?" Mary thought as she stood in the kitchen staring at the faded wall. "My man's going from bad to worse from anxiety to paranoia." She had shared about these experiences with her women's prayer group and nearly all there had thought that Mary needed to seek help for Robbie. The pastor agreed.

"This can't go on. Your man needs help and we will pray for him. He needs to see a counsellor," one of the women had said.

"Just be careful," warned another after they had prayed, "anyone these days can be a counsellor. This is a mental health issue so he needs the expertise of a clinical psychologist and I know just the one but he lives in Invercargill."

"Maybe he doesn't need anyone," suggested another woman. "I would have thought that it was quite normal to believe a treasure exists if a diver claimed to have recovered it. What reason would the diver have to lie about something like that?"

"It's a bit like those people who gamble at the casino," answered another. "They'll exaggerate about their winnings but never talk about their losses.

From what you told us this diver had a passion for finding wrecks with treasure and had been unsuccessful but, naturally, he doesn't want others to know this, so just maybe he made this whole thing up to feel good. After all, it's something that can neither be proven nor refuted."

"But would a person do this?" Mary thought. "I guess that this could be the case as a lot of people talk about their jobs as if they're important just to feel good."

Mary reached into the cupboard for the flour as she had planned on making scones. "No this can't continue, Robbie believing that there's gold when it clearly doesn't exist and now people are spying on him. At a guess probably some of his farmer friends wrote the ransom note after all a number of them are characters who might do that sort of thing. Robbie has been driving everyone up the wall and a response of this kind is overdue; deservedly a good ribbing as he is now starting to look very foolish. Colin, with all his grudges, hasn't helped by agreeing with him."

She stopped and sniffed then checked that her stove and oven were off as she could smell burning. The smell seemed to be getting stronger near the window and was coming from outside. She quickly left the kitchen and house to investigate. In the distance she could see smoke rising, then she saw the flames.

"Oh, my gosh! The barn's on fire."

She ran inside to the phone and called the fire brigade and was about to leave the house in search of Harry, last seen heading for one of the distant paddocks, when the door sprung open. Three people wearing balaclavas burst in, grabbing Mary by her arms.

"You're coming with us," shouted a female voice. Mary stood traumatised.

"Who are you? What do you want?"

They didn't respond as they tied her hands behind her back, gagged her, then roughly bundled her into the back of a station wagon like a sack of potatoes. They covered her totally with a blanket so she couldn't be seen by passing cars. It seemed like a half an hour's journey before the car finally slowed down. It now seemed to be passing over bumpy terrain, maybe a drive or paddock, Mary thought. Then it stopped with a bump.

She was blindfolded before being dragged out of the van and led into a house where this was removed.

"What do you want?" she managed to muffle under the gag as she was put on a chair.

"You know what we want, the gold," replied a woman wearing a balaclava. "We didn't want to do this but you gave us no choice. You've not made this at all easy for us."

"There's no gold, Robbie just got carried away. He's been going through grief," came a muffled sound from behind the gag. Mary now noticed that one of her captors was wearing her necklace.

"No gold, no freedom," replied the woman. "It's that simple." The three saw Mary tied up before leaving the room.

From the next room, she could hear the voices of three people arguing: two were women and the third was a man. Then she heard the outside door angrily being slammed. It appeared that the man had left in a huff as he screeched away in his vehicle.

Mary surveyed her surroundings. The room was no more than six square metres in size and had hinged windows which could easily be opened and used to escape if she could just get her arms free. But the rope was tightly wound around her wrists as she struggled to try and squeeze her small hands through. While her idea had merit, the rope was too tight. She looked around the room for anything which might help. Now she could hear women laughing in the adjacent room. It sounded like they might be having a cup of coffee or tea. Mary suddenly felt very thirsty. To think that this had all come about through Robbie's anxiety, sharing about gold that didn't exist. Yes, she would be getting a counsellor, this all had to stop.

Across the other side of the room, Mary noticed a table and on it lay a knife. If she could reach this then she could cut through the rope. But her legs were tied to the chair and her only hope was to rock the chair forward on each leg using her feet, where she could, to control the operation. Mary tried this approach and it seemed to work without making too much noise but she stopped as she realised that this might all be in vain. Once she reached the table, then what? How was she going to get the knife? Picking it up with her mouth off the table would work but she couldn't just drop the knife onto her lap or chair without the risk of stabbing her leg in the process. The knife might also fall onto the floor with the thud alerting her captors. Even if she managed to get the knife onto her lap there was still the problem that her hands were tied behind her back. There seemed to be no solutions as she continued to look around the room for alternatives.

The women next door suddenly stopped laughing and became very loud and aggressive.

"We can't and we won't," said one voice.

"Well, I am not leaving till we have the gold," she heard the other shout. "We've gone this far and we need to finish what we started."

"You can't."

Next thing the door burst open and one woman came storming into the room followed by the other shouting, "No don't do it."

"So, where's the gold?" the first woman screamed, looking at Mary. "I'm standing no nonsense, do you hear? You're going to tell me."

"There's no gold," was the muffled reply.

The woman slapped Mary across the face.

"Where's the gold?" The masked woman now started to pull Mary's hair. "You'll tell me one way or another."

"We don't have any," came a tearful Mary's reply.

"Stop it, no don't, Mum," the other woman pleaded.

The woman stomped across the room and picked up the knife from the table before returning to Mary.

"I can't imagine what it would be like to have one's throat cut," she said, holding it up by Mary's neck, "but you will tell me even if it comes to that."

"No, you can't. The gold's one thing but I won't be a party to murder," said the other woman. "Don't do it, Mum."

"Now where's the gold?" demanded the woman, again holding the knife to Mary's throat.

Chapter 26

"A knight in shining armour is a man who has never had his metal truly tested."

Anonymous

"I don't want your damn gold," stated Wally, who was now nursing his revolver on his lap. "What would I do with it at my age? Goodness gracious man, we're here to help you rescue your wife, Mary. Since you came to me in Bali I have been very concerned about your welfare and have had people keeping an eye on you. I suspected trouble was on the horizon and more importantly, I didn't want that little red notebook falling into the wrong hands."

"So the men on the beach at Bali were yours?" I asked.

"Yes, they were there for your safety. Bali can be a dangerous place, especially when you're flashing around a Rolex watch which is an open invitation to be mugged."

"And did you have someone watching us at Bali Collection?"

"Several."

"In Auckland?" I asked.

"Yes, do you recall a very large Samoan man? He was the first to come to your rescue and to call the ambulance."

"Gore?"

"Yes, that's how we knew where to find Mary."

"The drone?"

"I don't know anything about a drone," said Wally.

"Who are you then with all this surveillance at your fingertips and why is my welfare so important to you?" I asked. "And why did you lie to me when you went on a treasure expedition with my uncle and a diver named Andrew after being abandoned by Martha and my uncle?"

"Oh, you mean the Flor de la Mar expedition. A nice man that Andrew," Wally laughed.

"Yes, I need to confess that I wasn't that truthful when you asked me about your uncle's adventures, but it was a good yarn on a hot Bali day and was a bit of a laugh. I rather enjoyed it and had a few giggles later."

"It was all made up?" I looked angrily at Wally.

"No not all of it. This all happened many years ago. I just decided to spin a yarn or two at the same time." Wally cleared his throat.

"What do you know about the Flor de la Mar?" asked Wally.

"I know she was a Portuguese ship carrying treasure that sank off Sumatra," I replied.

"So, you've been talking to Andrew. Not just treasure, Robbie. What this ship was carrying is estimated to be worth 2.6 billion dollars, but the truth is that the ship broke up on a beach and the survivors were likely to have recovered most of it," replied Wally.

"Then why travel all that way to Malaysia if the treasure is no longer there?"

"Why indeed?" laughed Wally. "And why even bother diving there with the strong sea currents, near-zero visibility in the water and the muddy sea bottom?"

"Why?" I asked again.

"This was a treasure hunter's dream and more than enough to lure the greedy. Imagine finding all that wealth even though in reality it was never going to happen. Many others have tried and failed just like the General Grant. But it was a great cover for being in these waters, Andrew, being an innocent party just like Martha was, but after the Caribbean incident she became a liability and we could no longer use her." Wally gave a wicked smile.

"You've lost me," I said.

"Australia and New Zealand work closely together on defence matters," continued Wally. I worked for the Australian government and your uncle for the New Zealand government and in the bigger picture for the British and

Americans. You asked about the pirates' treasure. Initially, we were not a team of treasure-hunters as I led you to believe. Instead, we were what you might call spies, sent out to gather information on communist insurgents in the Malaysian islands. If you recall a lot was happening at that time with communists trying to get themselves established in South East Asia. But things did not work to plan as we were discovered and we were forced to flee to the sea with some of the communists in pursuit. We found a hiding place on a heavily bushed island where your uncle stumbled upon the pirates' treasure. It would have been nice if our superiors had kept the treasure part secret but they deliberately leaked the find to the media so we became famous as treasure-hunters — which made for a very good cover in our spy operations. But once it was leaked out we had governments and others all trying to claim what we had found and in the end, we had to pay off corrupt officials but managed to keep most of the booty and as you know became very rich. After this episode, your uncle's favourite saying was 'tell no one'."

"Yes, 'tell no one'," I replied. "He said that often."

"Now, with us being known worldwide as treasure-hunters, we were able to carry out diving for wreckage in the Black Sea and at the same time we were conducting spy operations in the neighbouring countries. There were many old shipwrecks believed to be in these waters, some dating back to the Greek and Roman empires and some amazing treasures have been found there."

"Where's the Black Sea?" I asked.

"Very important question as the location shows just how valuable our cover was. The Black Sea is surrounded by Russia, Bulgaria, Romania, Ukraine; countries at the time under Russian control. Then there's Turkey and Greece."

"That would have been around the Cold War between the Soviet Socialist Republic and the USA," I replied.

"Correct. But there was also tension between Turkey and Greece over the Mediterranean island of Cyprus. Maybe not of interest to Australia and New

Zealand but we also worked closely with the UK and USA in their areas of interest."

"I thought the USA had side-lined New Zealand after we refused our ports to any ship that was nuclear powered or carrying nuclear weapons," I said.

"All hype," Wally laughed. "It made a good cover for New Zealand operatives to do jobs for the Americans when Russians, Chinese and others thought our relationship was strained."

"Anyhow, then there was the Caribbean Islands which I touched upon in Bali," continued Wally. "We were assigned a job during the Cuban missile crisis and it was a bonus when we actually found a Spanish wreck with treasure off the coast to use as a cover. Martha went on many of our trips but was oblivious to the fact that these were spy missions. Our job involving Cuba was to meet up with an informant on the island, but it seemed like our cover might be blown when Carlos and his mates paid us an unexpected visit. I had no choice, they all had to die. Yes, I killed all of them and have no regrets. At the time when Carlos and his mates arrived, I was just about to bring up a large quantity of gold and silver coins. Your uncle and Martha didn't know about this. The next morning, after finding that your uncle and Martha had deserted me, I managed several dives and recovered a tidy fortune for myself. I would have spent much longer recovering more treasure but I knew that I needed to leave the area before the search party for Carlos arrived. He was an important man and if caught I would have died slowly."

"So the mission was a failure?" I asked.

"The Americans still got what they wanted. I'm afraid the U2 put us out of business," laughed Wally.

"U2, what's that?" I looked at Harry, and he too looked puzzled.

"The U2 Lockheed spy plane. It was used then and is still being used today. It took wonderful pictures of the Cuban missile sites. It flies at over 70,000 feet so you wouldn't even know it's there," laughed Wally. "It's so high that the pilots have to wear spacesuits."

"So, you aren't that worried about whether my uncle carried out a salvage operation on the General Grant and recovered gold?" I asked, changing the subject and remembering that we had been bundled into the vehicle as if we had no choice.

"Not at all. I have enough to keep me comfortable for the rest of my life," Wally laughed. "When you get older you find you don't need much in life, just your health."

"But that was such a long time ago — the spying. Why would the red notebook be of any use after all these years?" I asked.

"A long time ago, Robbie? Do you think so? You don't think a person in their eighties can still be an effective spy? I can tell you that the most unlikely people you'd think of are spies. Who's going to suspect an eighty-year-old man on a day or two's stopover in a Russian port getting off a cruise ship and having a look around as tourists do? It's so much easier getting into a country on a cruise ship than crossing a border with all their customs controls and police."

"Well, I'll be!" I replied. "So my uncle could have been working right up to his stroke?"

"Of course, but not a word to anyone," said Wally, looking sternly at me and Harry. "You're sworn to secrecy. So anyway where's that notebook? That's all I'm interested in and I think was what your uncle was hoping you'd bring me."

"I put that in a safe place in a bank vault," I replied.

"Good," replied Wally.

"You can have it providing you do me a massive favour and remove the revolver and fake passports as well. It was a bit of a worry wondering how I'd ever get that revolver out through a bank and back to Gore."

Wally and the other men laughed. "No trouble; we do that stuff all the time."

"We've arrived, Boss," announced the driver.

"Park the van out of sight," instructed Wally. "We'll walk down the drive."

"Wait" Wally pulled Harry and I back as the two men with guns in their hands moved quickly ahead down the drive towards the front door of the old wooden cottage. "We need to be sure that the place isn't being guarded."

Wally let us follow with him at a distance and as we drew closer to the cottage Wally's men burst through the door. We followed and entered the house.

"Mary!" I howled, as I saw the sight of her slumped in the corner of the room. She was sitting gagged on a seat with her hands tied behind her back. On one side stood a lady in a balaclava wearing Mary's necklace and next to her was a young lady.

"Mum!" yelled Harry, moving forward before being pulled back by one of Wally's men.

"Don't come any closer," said the lady holding a knife to Mary's throat.

"Drop it, Martha, it is me, Wally. You know what I'm capable of." Wally waved his gun. "And remove that stupid balaclava."

"Don't shoot," said Martha, removing the balaclava and looking across at Wally. "Is that you Wally, darling? You look much older but you're still very handsome and in great shape. They stole our gold and it's only fair that we get it back. I don't mind sharing it with you and am happy to go halves."

"Your share, Martha? You stole my treasure in the Caribbean, then left me to face those blood-thirsty Cubans out for revenge. Drop the knife or, I warn you, I will shoot."

Martha dropped the knife, knowing that Wally wouldn't ask twice. She burst into tears. "It's just so unfair after having done all that research to have somebody else steal it and take the gold."

I quickly ran over to Mary, first undoing her hands as I wasn't sure what she'd say once I removed the gag. Mary, however, had little to say to me as her mind was on other things. After Harry had finished untying her legs, glaring at Martha she walked straight across the room and in one swift motion roughly removed the pearl necklace from Martha's neck.

"That's my necklace, thief!" she shouted. "How dare you."

I chose my moment before walking across the room to Mary and hugging her. She burst into tears after having been through a traumatic situation and for a few minutes remained with her head pressed against my chest. About the same time, the door flung open and in walked Colin.

"You can put your guns down men, this is now a police matter. Otherwise, I'll be forced to lay charges for using firearms and probably illegal ones at that." Colin walked over to Martha. "I'll take it from here," he repeated, as he handcuffed Martha and the other woman who was still wearing a balaclava. "These are my prisoners and they'll accompany me to the police station."

"Thank goodness, I knew I could count on you Colin," I said. "Good to see that you're on the ball: first our barn fire and now the kidnapping. I guess not many traffic tickets issued today. You're a first-class policeman."

Wally and his men put down their guns and stepped aside.

"Not so fast, Colin," said Sergeant Smith, as she bounded through the door with two police officers in tow. "Colin here masterminded the whole thing; your assault, the floorboards, the stolen necklace and the kidnapping. I first became suspicious when we arrested the two villains in Auckland who assaulted you. We had them up on other charges but Colin deliberately screwed up the evidence for a return favour. After your assault we had very good evidence — the watch and ring, to put them away for a long time, so of course Colin they're now singing and it's not your favourite tune."

"Why?" I looked at Colin. "How could you betray a friend? We grew up together and more recently have spent many evenings together having a beer and trying to solve the world's problems and all this time you've been plotting against me?"

"Why? Because life's unfair, that's why. Your family stole our land and your uncle deceived my mother-in-law, stealing her research to find the General Grant. You owe our family at least several million dollars. We were simply trying to recover what is ours but no thanks to you we were forced into taking this action."

"But as I keep trying to tell you, Colin, there's no gold. You saw the barn burn down — no gold. We've searched the farm — no gold. How many times do I have to tell you that there's no gold?"

"There's no gold," repeated Mary, in tears. "I've been trying to tell everyone that now for some time but nobody listens. Nobody ever listens."

"You should have listened to the man, Colin, there's no gold. Take them away," ordered Sergeant Smith. Colin, his wife and mother-in-law were led out to the police car. "I'm so sorry about this, Mary and Robbie, especially as the villain was one of ours. I guess that we're no different to any other organisation, and now and again you get a bad one."

I passed Wally the bank key with instructions. "You'll remove everything from the box now won't you, then close off the safe rental?"

"You beauty, I will," replied Wally, snatching the keys out of my hand. "Have no fears, your worries are all over."

"Good, that is a weight off my mind," I said.

"I can drop you home," said the police sergeant. "Will you need any counselling, Mary?"

"No, just Robbie to make me a strong cup of tea when we get home and we can talk about when we're going to Thailand and Vietnam and maybe on a cruise or two. He owes me at least that."

Chapter 27

"There is gold everywhere, most people are not trained to see it."

Robert Kiyosaki

Back at the farm the police sergeant enjoyed the friendly welcome given by our dogs.

"I once had ambitions of being a dog handler," she said as she patted both dogs. After licks and pats were exchanged the sergeant came inside and joined us for a cup of tea.

"Well as I told you before Ka mua, ka muri," reminded the sergeant, as she looked at me.

"And what does that mean?" asked Mary.

"That we should look to the past to see the future," the sergeant explained.

"So you suspected Colin?" Mary suggested.

"Well, let's just say that I became troubled by a series of events where Colin was the common denominator, but tahi i wikitoria tatou," replied the sergeant, patting me on the back.

"Meaning?" I asked, turning to the sergeant.

"Together we overcame. You and Mary can now move on with life and put all your worries behind you."

"Good," said Mary. "It's certainly been a tough few months."

"Oh," said the police sergeant, smiling and passing me a gift, "the book which you left behind back at the station in your rush to get to the fire. You'll be speaking Te Reo Maori in no time."

"How wonderful, something Robbie has always wanted to do," lied Mary, smirking, who up to now had looked quite pale and washed out.

"Thank you," I managed with a grunt. There were far more important things to do on the farm like clearing away what was left of the barn than setting aside time to be learning another language, one I'd never use.

"Next time when you're in Auckland please drop by," she said as she rose from the table. "We'll be able to converse in Te Reo."

"Thank you but I don't know about a next time," I replied, "not after having been assaulted there." Mary though seemed to have other plans, and it seemed that we might have to stop there on route to a shopping holiday destination sometime soon.

"I'm sure that you'll get over it," said the sergeant as she left through the door.

"I'm off to investigate the barn," announced Harry, who had joined us to say goodbye to the sergeant.

"I'd dearly love to join you too to assess the damage, but I can't leave your mum alone in the house, not after what she's been through," I replied.

"Good man," said the police sergeant patting me on the back. "You're in good hands," she added turning to Mary as she got into her car.

Harry left the house at the same time as the police sergeant drove off. He was very keen to survey the damage now that the firemen had left. No doubt he was also eyeing up a few more trips to the metal merchant and dump lest I return to hoarding, starting with the roof metal from the destroyed barn. I watched Harry bound down the drive before I returned to the house with Mary. After all the trauma she needed me, even though she didn't want a fuss made. She was pleasantly surprised when I offered to cook tea.

"Thanks, dear, that's very kind and thoughtful after all these years of marriage," she replied, "but you don't even know how to boil water without burning the pan." I guess that she was right.

"Who can that be?" I said as a noisy motor vehicle pulled up outside the house. The dogs had started to bark but at the sound of a car door closing had gone very quiet. Now there came the sound of shingle going through a grinder and suddenly the door flew open and in walked our pastor.

"A cup of coffee?" Mary offered, her nerves initially on edge as the door had sprung open.

"I'll make it. Mary has just been through a lot of trauma and is in no condition." I rose and poured a coffee for the pastor.

"So I heard through the grapevine," said the pastor, putting his hand around Mary's shoulders and hugging her. "Can I say a prayer for you?"

A tearful Mary nodded and the three of us bowed our heads in prayer.

"Thank you," said Mary, as she wiped her eyes. "It was comforting to know that God was watching over me when I was gagged and tied to the chair. I knew in the end that things would work out."

"Yes, it's all about faith." The pastor took a seat and sipped his coffee. He passed a cursory glance towards the oven to see what was planned for tea.

"Yes, it has been a difficult time for Mary," I said, observing the pastor's body language, "so, I've offered to cook tea tonight. You're most welcome to stay," I added.

The pastor, almost spilling his coffee, replied, "Oh, that's very kind, Robbie, but as you know I have many parishioners on my list to visit, and Mary could do with a bit of space after what she's been through."

Mary looked tired and it would take time for her to work through this trauma. However, she managed to smile at the pastor's response.

"Oh, I met your man the other day. I thought that the name rang a bell and I discovered that he was the Jack I once shared a cell with. What a small world this is. I'm pleased that you gave him some work as the poor man has been through so much. It is so hard when you come out of prison because nobody wants to employ you."

"He's a very good worker," I replied, "and it was our pleasure. It just seemed odd that he wandered off."

"An unsettled spirit," replied the pastor. "He's just coming back to grips with life after time in prison and it will be some time before he settles down, but he agreed to come to church on Sunday."

"Church!" Mary almost choked on her cup of tea.

The pastor stood up, "Well I really must be going. It's a pity that there wasn't any gold as a bar or two would have come in very handy."

"I guess that if my uncle did find the General Grant treasure then it would all be well and truly spent by now," I replied, as the pastor walked out the door.

"Yes," murmured Mary. "There's no gold."

There was a lot more barking as the pastor drove away. Mary, who had now finished her tea, slowly rose to prepare the evening meal. It was just as she started to stroll over to the kitchen sink that Harry suddenly came bursting through the door.

"What is it?" Mary asked. "Can't you see that my nerves are already on edge, people bounding in without any warning? I've been through a traumatic situation, for goodness sake, in case you didn't realise."

"Sorry, Mum," said Harry. "It's just that I checked what's left of the barn and I'm afraid I'll have to make another trip to the metal merchant with all that old barn roofing iron, Dad."

"I thought so," I said, "but there should be some good pieces to keep out of that lot," I added.

"No, it's all going to the merchant, Dad," Harry said.

"So you rushed in just to tell us this?" Mary looked angrily at Harry.

"No, Mum, there's more." continued Harry. "The firemen ended up draining most of the lake to put out the fire but now the murky water, what's left of it, has finally cleared and I saw something at the bottom."

"Eels, I told you that there were eels in that mud-hole," said Mary.

"No, Mum, there's gold on the bottom, lots and lots of gold bars at the bottom! Dad, Mum, what do we do, this is so exciting? We've found the gold of the General Grant. It's true. It's really true."

"Has anybody else seen it, Harry?" I asked.

"No, Dad, because the waters got all stirred up and murky when they were drawing from the lake.

"Then tell no one, Harry. Tell no one," I said smiling.

At 12:51 am on Tuesday the 22ⁿᵈ February 2011, Christchurch New Zealand was struck by a major earthquake, levelling the CTV building opposite to where Brian Wilson was working. One hundred and thirteen lives were lost. This was the catalyst for Brian Wilson's writing career, and with my encouragement, he has published several books including, 'Moments in Time' and 'Bumpy Roads' which are very readable collections of short stories. In 2016 and 2017 the novels 'Operation Iran,' and 'The First Trumpet' followed. These received very good reviews.

I have been good friends with Brian Wilson for many years. As Kiwis, we both had a passion for overseas travel after our adventurous teenage years and at twenty-one, we first visited Australia together. Brian has since taken more daring trips including a trek through Northern Thailand where the only protection against communist insurgents, bandits and drug lords was the guide's machine gun. He also did six weeks of voluntary work in rural Zambia. In more recent times he has travelled with his wife throughout Europe and Asia.

Brian Wilson has an M.A. (honours) degree and worked as an investigator for thirty years. He and his wife of thirty-five years have three adult children and eight grandchildren.

David. R. Moore

Dear Reader,

I hope you enjoyed

TREASURE OF THE GENERAL GRANT

Please consider leaving a review on the Internet

Bookselling sites

Thank you